**'Lord Dalla**
**Micah enqui**

For a moment R̶̶̶̶̶̶̶̶̶̶̶ cup. 'It's *the* local social event of the year,' she explained.

'It would give me real pleasure if I could be your partner at the dance,' Micah said.

'I'd love to,' Ruth said. After a minute's companionable silence she added, half joking, 'You know you'll be seen as my partner, dining then dancing with me. In Bannick people think that's a definite commitment.'

'Let them think it. It could turn out to be true.'

She could think of no suitable answer.

**Gill Sanderson** is a psychologist who finds time to write only by staying up late at night. Weekends are filled by her hobbies of gardening, running and mountain walking. Her ideas come from her work, from one son who is an oncologist, one son who is a nurse and her daughter, who is a trainee midwife. She first wrote articles for learned journals and chapters for a textbook. Then she was encouraged to change to fiction by her husband, who is an established writer of war stories.

# COUNTRY DOCTORS

BY
GILL SANDERSON

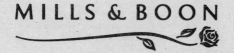

MILLS & BOON

*MILLS & BOON, the Rose Device and
LOVE ON CALL are trademarks of the publisher.
Harlequin Mills & Boon Limited,
Eton House, 18-24 Paradise Road, Richmond, Surrey TW9 1SR*

© Gill Sanderson 1996

ISBN 0 263 79536 5

*Set in Times 10 on 12 pt. by
Rowland Phototypesetting Limited
Bury St Edmunds, Suffolk*

03-9604-453195

*Made and printed in Great Britain
Cover illustration by Dewey Franklin*

# CHAPTER ONE

FOR the past hour the man had thought about nothing but his work. But now that he was saying goodbye to the woman framed in the train door he realised just how striking she was.

She was tall, six feet tall, and her belted blue mac hinted at slender shoulders and firm breasts. Her raven-black hair was long, but now tied up in a neat chignon. The severity of high cheekbones contrasted with the warmth of a generous mouth—but he noticed that she seldom smiled. This woman had a presence that went beyond mere beauty.

He said to her, 'And thanks again, Doctor. You know you saved his life.'

Ruth Francis gave one of her rare smiles. 'I was just there. A lot of other people could have done the same.'

'Possibly. But you were there and you did save his life. Have a pleasant journey.'

There was the shrilling of a whistle and the train eased slowly forward. The ambulanceman stepped away from the door and waved. Ruth waved back, closed the window then walked down the corridor to her seat.

It was one of those occasions when it felt good to be a doctor.

Luckily the train was half-empty. The ambulanceman had already found her a corner seat and slid her case underneath it. Ruth dumped her heavy briefcase on the table. Then, tucking her coat over her ruined tights, she sat, with a sigh of relief. The last hour had been eventful. She needed a minute to rest.

A heavy rainstorm was making the northern town even greyer and she gazed unseeing at the industrial wasteland flicking past. It was probably rain that had caused her to be delayed in the first place. And it was so little time ago. . .

The taxi had dropped her off just outside the station and she had hurried through the sudden squall into the shelter of the booking office. Perhaps there'd be time for a coffee before her train. Then, through the rattle of rain on the glass canopy, she'd heard the agonised scream of brakes. The silence straight afterwards had been equally dismaying. Ruth had grimaced. She'd known she'd have to check. Pushing the larger of her two cases against the wall, she had walked out into the rain.

On the other side of the road an old car leaned sideways, half on the high pavement. Nearby had lain a mountain bike, one wheel dreadfully crushed but the other still slowly spinning. And in front of the car a knot of people had gathered, their bodies in that strange stance that showed part curiosity, part anxiety.

Ruth had looked both ways before crossing the road. The scene of an accident was no place for careless behaviour. She'd glanced inside the car. The driver, a middle-aged man, had appeared shocked but in no immediate danger. She had walked to the small group of men and said decisively, 'Please let me through; I'm a doctor.'

Reacting to the note of authority, the group parted. The casualty was a young man, lying on his back, with another young man kneeling by him. Before kneeling herself Ruth looked up and down the recumbent body. The left leg was twisted and the man's trousers torn. There was some bleeding, but not enough to be immediately dangerous.

With a note of panic in his voice, the kneeling man said, 'He's not breathing! Shall I try to start his heart?' He placed his hands on the victim's chest.

Ruth hitched up her skirt and knelt by his side. Then she gently pushed his hands away. 'Please make sure that someone's sent for an ambulance. I'll take over now.'

Obviously happy to be relieved, the man stood up. All Ruth's attention was now on her patient. There was blood pooling behind his head; scalp wounds always bled heavily; it might not be too serious. But more important was the colour of the man's face. It was blue. Ruth leaned nearer; there was no sign of breathing.

There was no time for rubber gloves; carefully she opened the man's mouth and reached for his tongue. As she thought, he'd swallowed it. She eased it forward, freeing the passage to the lungs, and there was a sudden shuddering intake of breath. She smiled.

With one hand she clicked open her case. Like all her colleagues she always carried an emergency kit, including a plastic airway. Pulling off the protective cover, she eased it into the man's mouth and throat. He was breathing easily now, and already the blue colour was fading from his face. She took his pulse. It was fast, of course, but it seemed steady enough.

Ruth now felt cautiously at the back of the man's

head. There was a long gash and she reached for a pad to stop the bleeding. However, she felt it wasn't too serious. There was no simple way of telling if the skull, neck or spine was injured.

His leg was broken but the little bleeding there was came from superficial scratches. Ruth leaned back on her heels. She wasn't about to indulge in complex diagnosis or treatment in the middle of a city street. The man would now live until he got to hospital.

Through her thoughts she heard the distant wailing of the ambulance siren. It seemed no time before two paramedics in green high-visibility jackets were kneeling beside her.

'I'm a doctor,' she said briefly. 'I've put in an airway because he'd swallowed his tongue. There's a broken leg and scalp lacerations, possible neck injuries. Now I'll leave you to it.'

The paramedic team comprised a man and a woman. The man spoke. 'Thank you, Doctor. You will stay to give us a hand?'

'If you think you need me.' Ruth knew that this pair would be well trained and at least as competent as she in dealing with the initial stages of an accident. Stiffly, she climbed to her feet. 'I'll just check the car driver.'

She hadn't noticed the blue and white cars draw up, but the police were now efficiently taking charge, one man talking to the car driver while the others moved the crowd and spoke to the paramedics.

'I'm a doctor,' Ruth said to the policeman, feeling that it was a sentence she was getting heartily sick of. 'Is this gentleman injured at all?'

'I'm fine,' the driver snapped out, 'and I'd be a lot

better if I knew there weren't this many cyclists on the road. Don't they know that's it's slippery when it gets wet? That idiot. . .'

'No bruises, cuts or anything? You didn't hit the windscreen?' This was one of those times when she knew it would be more efficient to interrupt.

'I was belted up, like a good driver. I. . .'

'How d'you feel in yourself? No sickness, faintness or anything?'

'I feel angry; that's what I feel.'

The policeman turned and said reassuringly, 'I think we can look after him now, Doctor. If there's any doubt we'll take him to hospital.'

Ruth nodded briefly and returned to help the two paramedics gently lift their patient onto the stretcher. Quickly, it was slotted into the ambulance.

The woman went to drive and the man said to her, 'We'd like you to ride with him to hospital. Just to be certain?'

Ruth knew that it wasn't really necessary. But there was just one case in a thousand. . . She said, 'I left my case in the front of the station.'

Even as she spoke the ambulance, its siren sounding, was curving round to stop in the forecourt. Seconds later they were moving through the busy streets, traffic miraculously parting in front of them.

The driver radioed ahead to Casualty in the local main hospital and there was a doctor waiting as the ambulance drew up. Briefly, Ruth told him what she had observed, what she had done, what she suspected. 'And now I'm going to catch my train,' she finished.

He looked up, grinning. 'The emergency's over

now,' he said, 'but he was lucky you were there. Too many people like you roaming the streets and I'll be out of a job.'

'That'll be the day.' She noticed that even though he'd said the emergency was over he was eager to move the patient into the hospital. 'I'll leave him in your good hands.'

'We can run you back to the station,' the paramedic said, and fortunately there was a train due.

Now she was on it, and as she thought back over the past hour she felt vaguely pleased with herself. Yes, at times it felt good to be a doctor.

The ten-minute rest had refreshed her, and she remembered there was something she had to do. When kneeling on the wet road she had torn her tights; she'd better change them. She took a fresh pair from her bag and made her way to the little cloakroom. After changing she took the opportunity to comb her hair and check her minimal make-up. It wouldn't do for the Bannick locals to see their Dr Francis anything but perfectly groomed. In the country women doctors had to know how to dress.

There was a coffee-wagon passing as she took her seat again, so she bought herself a drink, then opened her briefcase and took out a sheaf of papers. There was work to be done.

For the past fortnight she'd been attending a course on new techniques in neonatal care. Her little country practice consisted of only three partners—old Dr Harry Crowder, his son, Martin, and herself. It was always hard for one of them to be absent, even though they all recognised that it was necessary to keep abreast of the latest developments. This time Harry had managed to get her free time, arranging for their trainee to start a fortnight early. Vaguely she wondered what he'd be like.

Ruth started to make notes. When there was time she'd run through the new ideas and techniques with her partners; it was important that they all profited by the course. And it had been a good course.

There'd been a lot to learn but also quite an exciting evening social life, based largely on the hospital club bar. She had met a few old friends, made one or two new ones. However, some of the GPs had obviously thought they could behave as if they were back in medical school again. Ruth frowned. It just wasn't her scene any more. She'd had to refuse several quite pressing invitations. She might be a widow but she didn't have to be merry. Ignoring the succession of bleak suburbs, she sipped her coffee and bent her head to her papers.

An hour and a half later she sighed and rubbed her forehead, feeling the beginnings of a headache. She'd had several lately. When she'd mentioned them to Harry his advice had been simple. 'You work too hard, you worry too much, you don't have enough interests outside the practice. Take things easier and relax a bit more.'

'I'll try, Harry,' she'd said, but she'd not been successful. She lived solely for her work. That, and the countryside surrounding Bannick.

She shut her eyes tightly for a minute, then opened them and glanced out of the window. They had long since left the last signs of industry and were running through rough pasture and moorland. It was still raining but there was peace and comfort in the great grey hills that etched a line against the sky. She smiled. She was coming home.

As she swept papers into her briefcase there was the faintest of tings as her fingers brushed the lock. She looked down. She still wore both the rings that Matt Francis had given her, wedding and engagement. The wedding ring was a simple band of gold; the engagement ring was unusual, a jade heart surrounded by tiny emeralds. She smiled sadly. Jade was supposed to symbolise peace and serenity. She'd loved Matt. But he'd brought her precious little peace.

If she looked out of the window now she could just catch a glimpse of Ironstone Edge. A week after it had happened she'd deliberately made herself walk past the cliff and she'd returned to it several times in the past six years. It hadn't been the cliff that had killed her husband. It had been Matt himself.

She shut her eyes, the wry smile still on her lips. It had been a lightning courtship and then a sudden marriage. Quite unlike the behaviour of the normally staid Ruth Applegarth.

She'd first met him in her last year at medical school when he'd been two years ahead. For some reason her friends had persuaded her to watch an inter-college rugby match. She'd known nothing about the game but even she could tell what kind of player the curly-headed forward was. He was mad. He'd run and tackled with boundless enthusiasm and no sense of danger.

Perhaps the result had been inevitable. He hadn't got up after one tackle and had to be helped off, with bleeding face and injured leg. As the trainer had helped him limp past he'd suddenly said, 'Doctor,' and had turned towards her. Thinking he might need help, she'd stepped forward. Before she'd known what was happening, he'd grinned, leaned forward and kissed her, full on the lips. 'I feel better already,' he'd said.

She'd had to laugh at his impudence, at the merry glint in his eye. But when he'd gone one of her friends had passed her a pocket mirror. There'd been mud and blood on her face where he'd kissed her. Only later had she thought it was symbolic.

As she'd studied that evening there'd been a tap on her door. It had been Matt Francis, face bruised and plastered, but still with that infectious grin. 'I'm sorry if I surprised you but not sorry I kissed you. May I buy you a drink to make up for it?'

She'd only been able to stammer, 'But. . .I was going to work. It's finals soon.'

'Rubbish. Saturday nights are for pleasure and partying. Too much work makes Ruth a dull girl.'

'Just enough work gets Ruth through her exams,' she'd said, but she'd gone anyhow.

After that evening she'd been swept along by his impetuosity. For some reason she'd abandoned her normal caution and had gone along with his madcap ideas. He never thought twice. His patients had loved him, even though too often he'd made mistakes.

They'd been married inside six months, for he'd refused to wait till she'd qualified. By great good fortune he'd found a junior registrar's post at a hospital twenty miles from Bannick; Ruth had been able to return to her home ground and take up the GP's job she'd always wanted.

Only he'd been in their little cottage when a phone call had come to say that a climber had fallen on

Ironstone Edge. He was badly injured, stuck on a ledge a hundred feet from the ground. Matt had reached the foot of the cliff minutes before the mountain rescue team. The accepted practice was very clear; the doctor had to wait till the experts came to assist him. Matt had never waited in his life.

He'd climbed the cliff, reached and treated the injured man. Then he'd slipped and fallen to his death.

Ruth shivered. Matt had died as he'd lived. And his death had made her more certain that her way of life was better—calm, cautious, methodical, slow if necessary. Fiery, erratic people only caused grief.

The train was now approaching Bannick, and every bend in the track revealed another well-loved scene. Here was the stream where she'd paddled when she was twelve. In the distance was the farm where a patient with heart trouble lived. Nearby was a row of cottages, in one of which she'd delivered a premature baby. Ruth sighed with contentment. She was coming home. She would settle back into her busy, well-ordered life where nothing unexpected ever happened.

'Evening, Ruth; have a good trip? Your car's outside and I've got the keys.'

She gossiped cheerfully with the stationmaster as he carried her bag. She'd been to school with him. Then she was travelling through the bustling streets of the small market town, home at last.

She felt in need of a bath and she wasn't expected at work till tomorrow. But she'd been away for a fortnight. She'd drop in at the surgery and pick up her mail.

The surgery of Crowder, Crowder and Francis was in a Victorian semi on the outskirts of town. It wasn't ideal but they managed at the moment. She frowned as she surveyed the vehicle-congested frontage. Definitely they'd have to do something soon.

She parked with difficulty. Most patients obeyed the large sign that said 'DOCTORS ONLY' but in her place was the newest Range Rover, in dark red. She looked at it with a mixture of envy and irritation. It was just the thing she needed in winter, when it was often difficult getting through to patients on outlying farms.

'Good evening, Mary,' she said to the receptionist as she entered. 'I don't suppose you know who's parked in my place, do you? I wish people would learn to read.'

Mary had been with Harry for thirty years, and knew everybody and everything. But she didn't answer, which wasn't like her. Instead she looked beseeching and rolled her eyes.

From behind Ruth a voice said, 'I must apologise, Dr Francis; it's my fault. But we weren't expecting you till tomorrow morning. Would you like me to move?'

Ruth loved the voice. It was deep, musical, with perhaps a touch of laughter in it. She had trained herself to listen to voices. Often a doctor would learn as much about patients from how they spoke as from what they said. And she loved choral music. She wondered if this man sang, perhaps. . .

The voice continued, 'My name is North—Micah North.'

She didn't want to turn round. His appearance couldn't possibly live up to his voice; it was bound to be a disappointment. But. . .

The voice went on, 'I'm your new trainee.'

'Our trainee?' she squeaked, whirling round. 'You can't be!'

'Sorry,' he said, 'but I am.'

'I'm Dr Francis,' she mumbled, and, for want of something to do, thrust out her hand. This man was not what she had expected as a trainee.

For a moment he held her hand firmly but his strength was controlled. He didn't need to squeeze. Too many men felt the need to impress a lady doctor by their handshake.

So far the practice had had two trainees, young doctors fresh out of medical school who needed experience before they could become GPs themselves. Both had been keen, able and willing to learn—but young. To the twenty-nine-year-old Ruth the twenty-three-year-olds had seemed almost comically youthful. But this man was older—she guessed somewhere in his mid-thirties. She decided that it was his age that had disturbed her. And she was definitely disturbed.

'I'm very pleased to meet you, Dr Francis,' he went on. 'I feel I know you a little bit already. I've been using your room.'

She wondered quickly if there had been anything personal or feminine left that could indicate her character, then decided not. Her consulting room was a work room. There was nothing individual in it at all.

He went on, 'And I've been addressed as Dr Francis three times and had to explain that, no, I wasn't taking over your job, and yes, you would be back soon.'

She smiled, recognising the typical Bannick reaction. 'I'm afraid many of our patients don't like change,' she said. 'They tend to distrust novelty.'

'They might well be right. Look, are you busy right now? I've been looking at the case notes of one of my—that is, *your*—patients and I'd like your advice. Of course, I'll have a word with Harry later but I'd like to talk to you.'

She appreciated the way he'd asked for advice. He hadn't looked as if he took advice from anyone. She said, 'I only popped in to say hello. I'd be pleased to have a chat.' He moved back to let her walk past him. Aware of Mary's not well hidden scrutiny, she entered the room.

As she passed him she realised just how tall he was. She had no problem with being six feet tall, though she'd met more than a few men who seemed to take it as a personal insult that she was a doctor *and* taller than them. But this man topped her by three or four inches.

They walked into her room. It seemed odd to her to be a guest in what she thought of as her territory. He must have realised her unease for he said, 'Now who is the important one and gets to sit behind the desk?'

The touch of humour relaxed her slight feeling of dispossession and she said, 'They're your notes on the desk, so you sit there.'

They both sat. He leafed through the papers on the desk and she seized the opportunity to study him covertly. After a while she realised that he too was glancing at her. Perhaps he was assessing her as she was trying to assess him? For a moment she wished she'd gone home and bathed before coming in.

He was a well-built, well-proportioned man. His dark hair was short and curly. At some time his nose had been broken and reset, none too well. It gave character to a humorous face. He was wearing brogues, grey flannels, tweed coat and a London medical tie with a white shirt, more or less the uniform adopted by the senior partner and his son. She appreciated that; he was trying to fit in.

But as she looked she realised that the clothes were much more expensive than those bought by Harry or his son. There was something about the fit of the jacket that suggested a very good London tailor. She felt a vague touch of unease.

He lifted his head, looking at her directly, and smiled. His eyes, she noticed idly, were large and a curious grey-green shade. Like the distant moors in early spring, she found herself thinking, then jumped at the fanciful thought.

'I know what you're doing,' he said. 'My old professor said that a GP's diagnosis starts with the medical card and carries on when the patient enters the room. You should watch him walk in, look round and sit down. Then you'll have some idea before he even opens his mouth.'

She blushed a little. 'Was I that obvious?' she asked.

He shrugged. 'Not obvious. But I was doing exactly the same to you.'

There was a pause for a moment that went on a little too long for Ruth's comfort. Then she shook herself. He might be older, but this man was her junior. In twelve months Harry would have to sign to state that he thought he was, or was not, fit to be a GP, and Harry would certainly consult her first.

'You've been on a course on neonatal care,' he said. 'Was it any good?'

This gave her a chance to be medical and efficient again. Quickly she mentioned the topics studied, the names of the lecturers involved. He picked up on one at once.

'I've heard of Professor Jim Lacey. He's got some radical new ideas on drug dosages for neonates. Are you thinking of trying them here?'

She frowned at his obvious enthusiasm. 'I don't think so. I know his results seem very good, but I'd like to wait a few years until he's done a bit more research.'

He said nothing for a moment, then, 'He seems to have managed one or two miracle cures. And with children who didn't have much of a chance.'

'I don't believe in miracles in medicine,' she said curtly. 'I think doctors—especially GPs—should be wary of wonderful new cures.'

He seemed unmoved by her rebuke. 'Are you going to talk to the practice about what you've learned?'

'Of course. When we can get together there are several things I feel we should discuss as a team. Perhaps one or two things we should change.'

'I'll be interested to hear,' he said.

She was still feeling a little unsettled and there was something she wanted to know. Bluntly she asked, 'Why are you training to be a GP? Have you worked in a hospital and decided it wasn't for you?'

He shook his head, unaffected by her question. 'Not at all. I've always wanted to be a GP. I graduated eighteen months ago and I've just finished a period in a central London practice. But I'd rather work in the country.'

She frowned. 'You only graduated a year ago? How old were you when you started training?'

Once again he seemed unaffected by her outspoken questioning. 'I left school at sixteen and worked as a clerk. But I always wanted to be a doctor. When I got the chance I studied at night school and I started medical school when I was twenty-six. I know it's unusual but it's not unheard of.'

'I see,' she said. She knew it wasn't unheard of. But most medical schools were very dubious about taking people so old. He must have had excellent A levels and put up a very impressive performance at interview to be accepted.

She felt there was something left unsaid. The man was unsettling. His answers, given so readily, seemed too bland. Then she decided she was being paranoid; she must be more tired than she had realised.

While she reflected he sat quietly, waiting for her to speak again. She remembered he'd asked to see her, some matter concerning one of her patients. 'Who d'you want to see me about?' she asked abruptly.

'William Knowles. I've got his case notes here and I've just been reviewing his history.'

When he offered them to her she waved them away. 'I know Billy Knowles. In fact I know the whole family.' Billy was aged sixty and still regarded the failure of his heart as a personal insult.

'Well, he was in two days ago, saying that now he couldn't even climb the stairs. He's not responding to treatment. I thought we might put him on an ACE inhibitor—Captoprial, perhaps?'

'No. The risk of renal failure is too great.'

'We'd have to monitor it, of course. But I've given him a blood test and we could watch the dosage.'

'I see.'

Ruth had to admit that there was much in what this new doctor was saying. But he was moving too fast.

Billy's present course of treatment might still work. And it was safe.

'I agree that Captoprial is a possible treatment,' she said carefully, 'but I think that Billy should stay with his present medication. He can cope; he's been coping for years.'

'He is your patient and it's your decision. But I'd like to explain the options to him, then let him choose. It would give him a chance of a better life.'

'I hate the word "chance"! It has no place in medicine.'

He shook his head. 'All life is chance. Every decision you make is a gamble. But that's no excuse for never taking a decision.'

That remark clinched it. She had it now. She knew why she'd felt increasingly disquieted by this conversation. He was a shadow of her former husband—a chancer. She looked at him warily. 'I see we're not going to agree. How about if we talk to Harry about it?'

He nodded promptly. 'Of course; he's my trainer. Don't forget I'm only the new boy; I'm here to learn.'

She could detect no touch of irony in his voice; apparently he meant it. 'Is there anything else?' she asked.

He shook his head. 'I've enjoyed the work so far.'

'Good.' She realised that so far their conversation had been entirely about work. She was a partner in the practice; perhaps it was time to welcome him formally.

'I'm sorry I was away when you started,' she said. 'I can see you're settling down to the work. But how do you find Bannick after London?'

'I like it; I like the people. I'm sure I'll be happy here.'

'Where are you staying?'

He waved to the local paper, open at the properties page. 'I'm still looking for somewhere semi-permanent. But for the moment I've got a suite at the Bell Hotel.'

'The Bell Hotel!'

'They've made me very comfortable there,' he said calmly.

Ruth thought this must be an understatement; the Bell Hotel was the most expensive in the town.

'Are you married, Dr North? I don't mean to pry, but if you have a wife we'd like to make her welcome.'

He shook his head. 'I'm not married and never have been.'

Now that's odd, she thought to herself. But he carried on, 'I understand your husband died in an accident some years ago, Dr Francis. I'm very sorry.'

Ruth shrugged. 'We're both doctors; we know these things happen.' But she thought he'd handled a difficult subject quite well. He was more mature than his predecessors. 'My name's Ruth, by the way. And you're Micah.'

'I am.' There was another short silence, more companionable this time. It was interrupted by a tap at the door and the cheerful face of Martin Crowder peered in. 'Saw your old car outside, Ruth. Welcome back. I see you've already met Micah. Both of you come and have a cup of tea with Dad and me.'

'That'll be nice, Martin.' She turned to Micah. 'We drink tea or coffee all the time here and talk—life's one continuous set of unofficial meetings.'

'That sounds nice. I like frequent cups of tea.'

'It makes us feel like we're all one happy family.'

It was meant as a careless, friendly remark. But

although his outward appearance didn't alter one jot she had the feeling that somewhere steel shutters were slamming down.

'I have no family,' he said bleakly.

# CHAPTER TWO

DRIVING to work the next morning, Ruth listened to a programme of Elizabethan love songs. 'Sweet maiden, let me be thy lover,' she sang along with the chorus. She liked the singer's rich baritone voice; it reminded her of—Micah North's? The moment that idea swept across her mind she reached forward and tuned in to Radio 4. There was no point in foolish thoughts. She'd see him in a few minutes. . .

She parked in her usual spot and noticed, with an unexpected thrill of interest, that the red Range Rover was already there. Then she spent a moment checking herself in the mirror; it wouldn't do for her to be anything less than perfectly groomed. When she knew that her chignon was tight, the faint touch of lipstick unsmudged, and that her rather severe blue dress hung properly, she stepped out of the car.

Even though she was early, the car park and the little waiting room were both full. She sighed. Things couldn't carry on like this. They would have to expand in some way. She shouted good morning to the office staff, who were coping as best they could with an avalanche of paperwork. Much of it, she knew, would eventually land on her desk. Then she tapped on Harry's door and entered.

He must have been reading her mind. He said, 'The days have gone when you could run a good practice out of a front room.'

Though Ruth agreed, she felt defensive. 'I think we provide a pretty reasonable service. People like us.'

'I know. That's why we take on more patients than we can fairly deal with.'

'We have to. We're part of the community.'

Harry smiled. 'I know you want to get back to work. Just serving notice. We'll have to have a serious talk soon.'

'Soon,' she agreed with a grin. Harry had been threatening this 'serious talk' for months.

'What I wanted,' she said, carefully casual, 'was to look through the trainee's application form. Isn't he a bit older than usual?'

Harry unlocked a drawer in his desk and threw a manila folder across to her. 'You read that while I throw most of my mail in the bin,' he said. 'Personally, I think we're lucky to get him. He's fitted in well here and the patients seem to like him.'

'Hmm,' she said, blue eyes dancing over the printed sheets. There was something wrong here.

Micah North's exam results were all excellent, even outstanding. His tutors couldn't speak highly enough of him. The previous year he'd spent in a central London practice and the doctor in charge had written an excellent reference. She frowned as she saw the address.

'Just where was he before, Harry?'

'You spotted it. Right in the heart of Belgravia. That must be one of the richest practices in London.'

'So why did he come to the impoverished north?'

'I asked him that. He said he'd always wanted to work in the country.'

'And you say he's worked well so far?'

'Perfectly. Neither over-confident nor scared to

make a decision. He hasn't brought any big city ways with him. He wanted to try a new course of medicine—a bit experimental, perhaps—with that young Stather girl. We talked about it for quite a while. He'd spent some hours in the library reading up on the treatment and he was able to convince me that it was worth a trial and so far it seems to be working.'

'Hmm.' She handed back the manila folder and went to her room. Time to start work. But something still troubled her. Micah North could have had his pick of hospital or GP placements. Why had he elected to come here? She loved the little town, but she knew most people thought it was a backwater.

It was good to get back to her familiar room and deal with the usual litany of complaints. Most of the people she'd met before and she knew when she had to dispense advice and reassurance as well as prescribe medicines.

The summer season was just about starting and there were two or three emergencies from holiday-makers. A cheerful young lad with an obviously painful burn from a camping stove was sent for a Flamazine dressing. She prescribed Imodium for one or two upset stomachs. More serious was a one-year-old baby suffering from diarrhoea. She prescribed dioralyte sachets, explained how to mix them with boiled water and told the anxious parents that she'd call round that evening at the caravan site where they were staying.

Then the last patient was seen, the last card placed on a pile on the desk. She stood and stretched. It was good to be back in harness.

Whenever possible Harry liked his fellow doctors to meet for lunch and a general talk. Ruth thought it a good idea; it was surprising how many times she'd been able to solve problems after listening to other people. They sat casually in Harry's room, drinking coffee and eating sandwiches. She looked forward to it after morning surgery.

Today, of course, there'd be a new member: Micah North. She felt a little dart of pleasure at the thought. Then she felt dismayed, and reassured herself that she was solely interested in him for professional reasons.

She slid quietly into the room and poured herself coffee from Harry's wonderful new machine. Harry and his son Martin were arguing loudly over some business matter. Both waved cheerfully but neither stopped talking. Micah stood with his back to her. He had opened Harry's beautiful mahogany bookcase and was intent on one of the leather-bound volumes there.

Happy not to be observed, she stared at him. Once again he was wearing the accepted dress of the practice, a different tweed jacket today, flannels and brogues. The jacket was in a brown tweed she'd never seen before, managing to look both rich and sombre. Once again Micah's clothes were expensive.

As she realised this, she realised something else. Micah's eyes weren't on the book he held. Instead they were fastened on the open glass door of the bookcase. While she had been staring at him, he had been staring at her reflection. Why?

He closed the book, turned, and stepped towards her. Sitting in the chair next to hers, he tapped the book and said, 'I've just been looking at this directory of Bannick in the 1850s. I recognise quite a few of the names from our patient lists.'

'You'll probably find my family name there,' she

said, happy to talk about some non-personal subject. 'We've been here for ages.'

He flipped the book open. 'I've found you already. Adam Applegarth, wool merchant.'

'How did you know I was an Applegarth?' she asked, slightly disturbed at his knowledge.

He grinned. 'Round here you still are an Applegarth. I had at least three patients last week who asked for "young Ruthie Applegarth". One of them was your old primary-school teacher. We had quite a chat.'

'Miss Ledgard,' Ruth said, and forced herself not to ask what the chat had revealed.

'What I was vaguely wondering,' he went on, 'was if there were any problems here to do with long-term intermarriage. I mean, a couple of recessive genes and a little town this size could be in trouble.'

At first she resented the implication. This was her town; there was nothing wrong with it. Then she realised it was quite an interesting question. 'I don't think so,' she said slowly. 'Perhaps there might have been more trouble in the nineteenth century, but even then this was a market town and there were traders visiting from all over the north.'

Harry had heard the last couple of sentences and joined in the conversation. 'I'd agree with you, Ruth, about Bannick. But I think the same might not be true about one or two of the surrounding villages. What about Lesteril?'

'Lesteril!' Ruth grimaced. It was a dirty little village. They had a large number of patients there who suffered from ill-defined complaints and who would never follow a course of medication through to the end. They were now nearly all resistant to antibiotics.

'They all intermarry in Lesteril,' Harry pointed out.

'Largely because no one else would have them,' Martin put in, cruelly but not inaccurately.

Micah kept quiet during this exchange, but Ruth had the feeling that he was listening and noting. 'It is quite an interesting thought,' she said. 'Perhaps Lesteril's problems *are* due to inbreeding?'

'Run the case histories over the past fifty years through a computer and you might come up with some significant conclusions,' Micah put in.

Martin winked at Ruth. 'We've got a super-efficient computer in the hall. It's Mary. I'll just ask her what she thinks.'

'You could do worse,' Harry said drily. 'I think you've got an interesting point there, Micah. But it'll have to wait until we get the entire practice computerised.'

'Just a thought,' Micah said calmly.

Harry had taken a piece of paper from his pocket and was considering it through his half-moon spectacles. Ruth recognised it as one of the notes that he frequently wrote to himself. 'Ruth, would you like to go out to High Walls Farm and have a look at old George Miller?'

'Love to,' she said promptly. 'Nice to see George and I fancy the ride. Is his heart worse?'

'Not that we know officially. I met his son, young George, in the market on Saturday. He says his dad is as awkward as ever but at long last doing what we told him to—taking things easy. Now that worries me.'

'I know what you mean.'

'So just drop in. And why don't you take Micah

with you? You can show him where our outlying patients live.'

Her heart thumped. Take Micah with her! Of course it was a good idea; there was a lot she could tell and show him about the district.

'Would you like a trip in the country?' she asked, almost shyly.

'I'd really enjoy it,' he said imperturbably. 'Shall we start at once?'

'And Ruth,' Harry called as they walked out, 'if Mrs Miller gives you a box of eggs, I want half.'

'Medicine in the country,' she explained to Micah, 'sometimes has its advantages.'

He suggested that since he needed to get to know the local roads they should take his car. She agreed; secretly she rather fancied a ride in the luxurious vehicle. He gave her the keys to get in while he fetched his case.

Inside, the car was lavish. She relaxed in the hide-covered front seat, drank in that smell that only new cars had. It was a contrast with her stolid Ford Escort.

There was a rack of tapes below a complex-looking music system. Curiously she bent over to look through them; you could often. . . The driver's door clicked open and she looked up, disconcerted. Micah, how-ever, seemed happy that she should want to search through his collection.

'Pick a tape,' he urged as the powerful car surged through the gate. 'I hope you can find something you like.'

She shook her head. 'Not yet. To be frank I wanted to see what kind of music you like. If you can tell a person's character by the books on their shelf, then you should be able to do the same by the tapes they choose.'

He laughed. 'Does it always work? Is it a safe diagnostic technique?'

'Well, Martin's car's full of tapes of fairy stories— but they're for his children.' She paused a moment. 'That is, I hope they are.'

They both laughed. 'Look through,' he said. 'I bought those tapes to please no one but myself.'

'All right.'

Her first reaction was to notice that all the tapes were expensive; there were none of the cheap compilations people bought in motorway shops. That suggested that he chose his tapes carefully—and so the choice made him a very odd character.

'Well?' he asked as she stretched upright. 'Conclusion, please, Doctor.'

'No doubt about it. Mostly Mozart, some Bach and Beethoven, but then "Songs for Swinging Lovers" by Frank Sinatra, and a collection of hits by Eartha Kitt. Split personality. You're an obvious schizophrenic.'

He laughed again. 'There are times in the car when only Frank Sinatra will do.'

She felt a sharp stab of irritation as she wondered about this. Presumably he meant when he had a female companion with him. She wished she could ask him why he'd never married, but decided she didn't know him well enough yet.

They'd now turned out of the little town and were heading along B roads towards the steep slopes to the north. He drove much faster than she thought safe, the tyres squealing on the bends.

'Would you mind driving a bit slower?' she asked

cautiously. 'I'm not used to this speed.'

'I'm quite safe,' he said, 'but I'll certainly slow down.'

He did so, and she felt like a wet blanket. Then she decided she had no reason to; there was no reason to be ashamed of not liking excess speed. If it was excessive.

'Have you lived here all your life, Ruth?'

It was the first time he'd called her by her name; it gave her an odd shock. 'All my life except for when I trained in London,' she admitted, 'and my ancestors lived here before me.'

For a moment he took his eyes from the road to look at her and she felt pleased at his obvious admiration. 'I've been reading a bit of local history. The Vikings settled here first, though it seems a long way from the sea. I think I can see something of the Viking in you. Those high cheekbones—they're gorgeous.'

She felt her heart lurch. No one in Bannick had ever called her gorgeous. It wasn't a word dour northerners used. For a moment she felt a slight touch of panic. This friendship—or whatever it was—was moving too fast. She decided she'd have to talk about something else.

'Why did you want to work in the country, Micah?' She realised it was the first time she'd used *his* name. It seemed like the beginning of some new kind of intimacy, another step forward in their relationship. She went on, 'You got a very good reference from the doctor in London. And you've lived there all your life.'

'You've seen the reference?' he asked, surprised.

'I'm a partner in the practice. Of course I've seen it.'

Although he said nothing Ruth got the impression

that he wasn't pleased at her knowing about him. That was too bad; she had her job to do.

But when he did speak his voice was perfectly pleasant.

'When I was small my great-aunt Molly used to take me on day trips to the village where she'd been born. It was in the Weald. I got this impression of big skies, big fields with flowers, quietness. I knew that when I grew up I wanted to live somewhere like that. Well, I did grow up and I still feel exactly the same.'

He went on, 'That's a personal feeling. Professionally, I think London's too full of people and they're all in a hurry. More than half my patients I only saw once. There was never any chance to establish a relationship. I wanted to work where I could get to know people.'

The great car pulled out to overtake someone on a bicycle; Ruth turned to wave. 'Getting to know people is two-edged,' she said. 'People also get to know you. That was Albert Day on his bike and he dearly loves to gossip. Tonight someone in the village where I live will ask me who I was out with. In the country everything you do is noticed and commented on.'

'So you can't let your hair down when you want to?'

She wondered why he was asking. 'It's no problem,' she said flatly. 'I neither need nor want to let my hair down.'

She felt rather than saw his amused glance, and for something to do leaned forward to rummage through the tapes. 'May I pick one?'

'Whichever you like.'

As the sounds of Beethoven swelled through the car she wondered if he'd realised that she just wanted to stop the conversation for a while.

As they drove she noticed that, although he kept a keen eye on the road, whenever he could he looked at the peaks that were now crowding in on them. An appreciative half-smile showed how much he liked the surroundings. Feeling a bit like a tour guide, she started to name the hills as they passed.

'And that's the Ferris Ring,' she said, pointing to one side. 'It's a really good ridge walk because you finish only half a mile from where you start. The views from the top are tremendous but it only takes about an hour and a half.'

'It looks good; I'd like to try it. Do you walk much, Ruth?'

She felt defensive. 'When I can. But usually I find something urgent stops me.'

'I know the feeling.'

They were now approaching High Walls Farm and she directed him first down a narrow lane and then onto a rutted path. Above them they could see the farm, perched on the edge of the steep valley side.

'My little Ford can only manage this in dry weather,' she said. 'In winter I just pack a pair of wellies and walk from here.'

'Let's see what this wonder machine can do.' He engaged the differential lock and they raced up the track at what seemed to be an alarming speed.

'You seem very competent,' she said dubiously, hanging on as they bounced round a bend that was both steep and sharp.

'When I bought this I went on a course on cross-country driving. I thought it might be useful, even though it's not a normal part of a doctor's training.'

'Quite,' she said as they lurched into the farmyard. He seemed to think of everything.

Before they entered the house she told him about George Miller. As so often happened with patients, the family background was just as important as the medical details.

'This farm's been in George's family for years. George was born here; he says he intends to die here. He worked an eighteen-hour day for years on end and the place is now very successful. Two years ago he had a triple bypass. We got him to hospital in time and he pulled through. But. . .well, what would you say?'

Micah answered promptly. 'If you want to carry on living, then you need a complete change in lifestyle.'

'Right. In fact George's eldest son now runs the farm and so far he's just managed to stop his dad from overdoing it. But now old George isn't even trying to work, and that's why we're worried.'

First it was necessary to have a few words with Mrs Miller in the kitchen and say that, yes, they would like a cup of tea. Then they walked into the stone-flagged living room. George was hunched by the fire and Ruth could tell at once that something was wrong.

'Morning, George. This is Dr North, who is working with us just now. How are you today?'

'Young Ruth Applegarth,' George said, ignoring the question. 'Women shouldn't be doctors.' Looking at Micah, he said, 'You're not from round here?'

'No. I'm afraid I'm a Londoner, born and bred.'

'Ah. You've come up here to work with us simple people?'

Micah grinned, not at all put out. 'If you're simple then dry-stone walling's easy.'

'What d'you know about walling?'

'Not a thing. Ruth pointed out what you'd done as we came up the hill. D'you think you could lie on the bed so we could have a look at you?'

'I don't like being poked about.' But even so he went to his bedroom.

Both Ruth and Micah listened to George's chest, and Ruth gave him a swift but competent examination. They could find nothing wrong, but George was obviously not well.

'Young George says you've not been getting about so much,' Ruth suggested.

'I'm just doing what you told me to. What more d'you want?'

'No other pains to tell us about? No discomfort of any kind?'

'I tell you I'm all right!'

Both Ruth and Micah had noticed an almost imperceptible hesitation before he spoke. However, looking at that wooden face, Ruth knew she'd never get him to tell her anything he didn't want to.

'Why don't you nip along to the kitchen and see how Mrs Miller is getting on with that tea?' Micah said. 'Perhaps George would like a cup as well.'

She could hardly believe what she was hearing. This man was the trainee, and he was trying to dismiss her as if she were a junior nurse. She wasn't going to argue in front of a patient but Micah North had better understand just who was in charge here. Then George said, 'I wouldn't mind a cup, Ruth.'

She looked across the bed at Micah's bland face then walked to the kitchen.

When she returned, leading Mrs Miller, who carried

the tray, Micah offered her a piece of paper. 'This is what I would prescribe, Doctor. Do you agree?'

Trying to conceal her anger, she looked at the scribbled word—'Fluoxetine'. Realisation flooded through her and her anger was turned back on herself. She should have known. It was nothing to do with George's heart; he was suffering from depression. Micah had guessed and, more than that, he had realised that George didn't want to talk about it to someone whom he still thought of as a schoolgirl. Ruth felt a fool.

'It's quite an exciting prescription,' she said guardedly, 'but I'm sure it will do the trick. And now I'm ready for that cup of tea.'

As they bumped back down the path from the farm Ruth clutched two boxes of eggs. Mrs Miller had been very particular to give them one each. Micah seemed to have made an impression on the woman. He'd also made an impression on Ruth. He was obviously a good doctor.

'I should have spotted that depression,' she said hesitantly. 'It was bright of you to realise that he didn't want to talk to me.'

Micah shrugged. 'You'd have got it in a couple of minutes,' he said. 'I'd expect you to be quicker than me in detecting something that was specifically female.'

She didn't think this was true, but she appreciated the way he'd found an excuse for her. 'May we listen to the rest of that Beethoven?' she said.

They hardly spoke on the journey back but it was a companionable silence. Ruth was quite happy to listen to the music. For the moment she neither wanted to talk nor to think. She was content to let things happen.

Soon they were back at the surgery. As he swung out of the car, he turned to her and said, 'I know it was work but I thoroughly enjoyed our little outing.'

She felt foolishly confused. 'I enjoyed it too,' she said.

Surprisingly there wasn't much work for the rest of the day and she arrived back at her cottage reasonably early. She hadn't seen Micah again; he'd been helping Harry with something.

Sure enough, someone had seen her, in a new Range Rover, with a young man.

A neighbour called across. 'Our Albert saw you out driving, Ruth.'

Ruth recognised the unspoken question. 'We've got a new doctor,' she said, 'I was just showing him round.' Then she slipped inside to avoid further chat.

The cottage was in Whiston, a village about four miles from Bannick. She and Matt had bought it, intending to live there for just a couple of years until they could find something bigger. After his death she had decided to stay; she had been happy there and she wanted to live with her memories.

She placed a small pile of letters on the mantelpiece, to be attended to later. On the corner of the mantelpiece was her favourite picture of Matt, as a young medical student, sitting on a bed, grinning happily.

After the accident she had placed the picture there and it had comforted her, as if some part of him were still alive and in the room with her. Now she realised she didn't look at it as often as she used to. She knew that grief must and would pass. Picking up the picture, she also realised that she knew exactly what he'd say to her if he could. 'Life must go on, girl. Go and live it.' She sighed. In a way she would always love Matt. But. . .

She'd picked up on Micah's bleak remark about having no family and she wondered if there was any tragedy in his life. Perhaps it was something they had in common. In time she'd know him well enough to ask him. But not yet.

She decided she was thinking too many unsettling thoughts; she'd had too much time in the grey city. She didn't want to do any of the many tasks that called her, and instead decided she'd get some reviving exercise. Ever careful, she left a message on her answering machine stating where she was going. Then she rushed upstairs and changed into her walking gear.

It was a couple of years since last she'd walked the Ferris Ring but seeing it with Micah had brought it back to mind. It was the perfect evening walk. It only took twenty-five minutes to drive to the little Forestry Commission car park and then she was striding up the steep slope that led to the ridge.

As ever, the physical exercise relaxed her. She reached the first summit out of breath but exhilarated. After a moment's pause to admire the vista of peaks and valleys, she set off along the ridge.

The path connected four peaks, known as the stones in the ring. She could see each one; the path stretched out in front of her and then curved round in a great sweep to her left. She had been walking for twenty minutes when she realised that she was not, as she had thought, alone. In the distance there was a small figure moving towards her. For a moment she felt a childlike twinge of annoyance; this was her country and she wanted to be alone.

She walked on, taking pleasure in the changing landscape, the bird-calls, the weak warmth of the sun on her face. The path undulated gently, so that every now and again she could see the figure walking towards her. Perhaps another twenty-five minutes passed before the first suspicion flashed across her mind. It was something to do with the way the figure walked. Five minutes later she was certain. Micah North was walking towards her.

The firm realisation that it really was him brought about a turmoil of battling emotions that shocked her by their intensity. First there was anger. She'd come up here, she now realised, to avoid thinking about Micah. It was wrong of him to force himself on her like this. Then the sheer injustice of the idea made her smile.

Perhaps she could drop down off the ridge on one of the smaller paths? But why should she? Anyway, now he had seen and recognised her; she returned his enthusiastic wave.

Reluctantly she now recognised the second emotion she was feeling. She was looking forward to seeing him. Forcing herself to be painfully honest, she had to admit it—there was no one she'd rather meet here by accident.

Inexorably they moved towards each other, catching glimpses as the paths twisted. Then they were together, meeting on a small heather-covered terrace.

'Ruth, how nice to see you,' he greeted her. 'If I'd

known you were coming out here we could have walked together.'

'It was a last-minute thing,' she said. 'I just felt the need to get away.'

'It's certainly a wonderful walk. I must thank you for telling me about it.'

'I like it too,' she agreed.

It was the first time she'd seen him not wearing his customary doctor's outfit. Instead he wore dark blue breeches and a red anorak. Everything he wore seemed brand-new—unlike her own kit, which had the happy shabbiness of much use. She looked at the small insignia on the jacket; it was as she had guessed. The very top of the range. Micah North certainly believed in buying the best clothes.

He looked at her thoughtfully. 'Shall I turn round and walk with you or do you want to be alone? Please don't hesitate to say so. I often like being alone myself.'

'I'd be glad of your company,' she said, discovering that this was entirely true, 'but I'll turn round. I've done the walk before, and it's your first time.'

'Right, then, if you're sure you don't mind.'

She was pleased that he'd accepted her offer. They walked back, and she acted as his guide, pointing out walks he might like to try another time. Much of the time, however, they were silent. For some reason they didn't talk about anything medical or personal; it was as if they had an unspoken agreement to keep the conversation light.

It was dusk when they reached her car again and he pointed out the lay-by half a mile away where he'd left his car. 'D'you live near here?' he asked.

'At Whiston, about ten miles away,' she said. She'd

been wondering about how they'd say goodbye and had decided against asking him back for coffee. She guessed he might invite her for a drink at the nearest pub so she quickly went on, 'I feel really tired so I think I'll go home and straight to bed. I've had a wearying fortnight.'

'I'll say goodnight, then. I've really enjoyed the walk—and your company.' Gently he put his hand on her arm, then turned and strode down the road. Ruth held her arm where he'd touched her and watched his disappearing figure. As ever, she'd been cautious. For once she was regretting it.

# CHAPTER THREE

'MARTIN'S off,' Mary greeted Ruth the next morning. 'Phoned in to say he thinks he's got this flu that's going round. You're picking up a third of his patients.'

'And that's all we need,' Ruth groaned. 'All right, Mary, if there's anyone in the waiting room I'll begin at once.'

After that the rush started. She lost count of the number of times she had to explain that influenza was brought on by a virus, not a germ, that there was no instant cure for it, that the only treatment was aspirin, rest in bed and plenty of fluids but no alcohol. There were one or two cases that needed a follow-up call and she knew the next few days were going to be hectic.

She was late when she finally got to Harry's room for her midday coffee. 'It's been one of those mornings,' she announced, collapsing into a chair. 'How's Martin, Harry?'

'Feeling too sorry for himself to feel sorry for us,' Harry said breezily. 'I'll call in on my way home tonight.'

Micah turned from where he had been bending over the coffee machine. 'You obviously need an infusion of caffeine,' he said. 'Doctor's orders that you take sugar with it this time.'

'That might be a good idea,' she agreed. He brought it over for her, their hands brushing as she took the cup. For a moment a memory flashed, bright as silver, of the way he had looked at her the night before. Then it was gone, and they were medical colleagues again.

'I've been on the phone checking round a bit,' Harry went on, 'and it looks like we're next in line for this flu mini-epidemic. Fortunately it doesn't seem too serious and it only lasts three or four days. But we're going to be busy, and there'll be more than the usual number of night call-outs.'

Turning to Micah, 'I hope you haven't organised a full social life for the next week?' he asked cheerfully.

Micah shrugged. 'I'm more than happy to rally round. In fact, while I'm doing nothing much at the Bell you two both have homes to look after. I'll take over Martin's share of the night calls.'

'That's very good of you but there's no question of it,' Harry said. 'We're a practice; we share everything.'

'But I need the experience,' Micah said artfully. 'Honestly, Harry, it's no great problem for me.'

'Well, perhaps an extra evening. . .' Harry weakened.

'It's settled, then.'

'I'll bet Martin will be back in three days at the most,' Ruth put in. 'He's done the sensible thing in staying off.'

'Let's hope you're right.' Harry beamed at his two colleagues. 'Now there's something a little more pleasant. In a fortnight it's Lord Dallan's summer ball and we've been allocated three double tickets. Can we get up a party? I—'

There was a tap on the door and Mary's disapproving face appeared round it. 'Dr Harry, there's a salesman here says you promised him exactly five minutes.'

'So I did, Mary. Excuse me, you two, for exactly

five minutes.' Harry gulped his coffee down then left.

'Lord Dallan's summer ball?' Micah queried gently.

For a moment Ruth took refuge behind her cup. She felt apprehensive, largely because she did not know exactly what she wanted herself. 'It's *the* local social event of the year,' she explained. 'Round here tickets are like gold. Lord Dallan opens his house for a ball and all the proceeds go to Kilham Hospital League of Friends. Lord Dallan, incidentally, is always too busy making money in London to attend.'

There was a pause for a moment and then he said, 'Harry and Martin will obviously take their wives. You're the third real member of the practice; you'll have the third ticket.'

She shook her head vigorously. 'I've been before; I don't particularly want to go again.'

Gently he asked, 'There's no one you want to go with?'

'No, you go; I'm sure you can find a partner.'

'I could probably find someone from London,' he said, and she suffered a pang of resentment that dismayed her in its intensity.

'However,' he went on, 'I know it's the obvious thing to do and I know people will expect it. But it would give me real pleasure if I could be your partner at the dance.'

She tried hard to conceal her pleasure at the curiously old-fashioned request. She wondered if she was making the right decision; this wasn't the normal reclusive Ruth Francis. Then, 'I'd love to,' she said.

Harry was delighted with their decision and said he would book a table for six at once. 'That's only for the dance,' he explained to Micah. 'Martin and I have family arrangements to make; we can't manage the dinner.'

'There's a dinner?' Micah queried.

'There certainly is. In the grand banqueting hall, all very swish.'

'I want to go to the dinner as well,' Micah said firmly. 'You do, don't you, Ruth?'

For the first time in years Ruth felt that someone else was making decisions that perhaps she ought to make. 'Well. . .' she said.

'I don't think I've ever dined in a grand banqueting hall,' he said plaintively.

'Poor deprived child,' she mocked. 'All right, Cinderella will go to the dinner as well as the ball.'

'I promise to polish my buttons.'

For a while they talked about more general medical matters, then Harry excused himself while Ruth and Micah finished their coffee.

After a minute's companionable silence she said, half joking, 'You know you'll be seen as my partner, dining then dancing with me. In Bannick people think that's a definite commitment.'

'Let them think it. It could turn out to be true,' he said.

She could think of no suitable answer.

For a week they hardly saw each other, smiling hastily as they passed in the corridor or as they gulped their coffee. Martin did return after three days but he was far from well, and Micah took his night duties. But then things calmed down, and as often happened there was a period with little to do.

'The sun's shining,' Micah said to Ruth one lunchtime. 'I've got no calls to make so if you're going into the country again I'd like to be your chauffeur.'

'I'd welcome the company,' she said, shyly pleased, 'and I can always play more of your tapes.'

'Let's go, then.'

She wondered if their conversation would be as memorable as their last trip together but for the first half of the journey they chatted inconsequentially about the countryside.

Ruth now thought she knew why he had come to work here. As he looked out of the car window there was a contentment in his eyes, a delight in the ever varied scenery. He looked at home here.

After half an hour they found themselves at a farm at the head of a lonely valley, and Ruth went inside to talk to Millie Carson, the farmer's wife, a woman prematurely aged by arthritis. She knew there was little she could do apart from prescribe pills, but a friendly visit and an examination showed Millie that someone still cared.

'I know it's not a killer,' she said as they drove back down the valley, 'but I sometimes think that arthritis causes more misery than any other disease.'

'An interesting thought. I wonder if—? Look, is that man waving to us?'

She craned her neck to see where he was pointing up the valley side. Down across a steep paddock a man was running, waving frantically. Micah switched off the engine and faintly Ruth could hear shouting. 'Doctor! Doctor, stop!'

They watched, amazed, as the man fell and rolled a few feet, then picked himself up and ran again. 'He's going to break his neck if he's not careful,' Micah said. 'We'd better see what he wants.' Engaging the differential lock, he bounced the heavy car off the road and drove up the steep, grassy slope.

'You're doctors,' the man panted as they reached him. 'Please, it's my daughter; I think she's dying. She was all right an hour ago but she's stiff and—'

'Get in,' snapped Micah, reaching to open the back door. 'Where is she?'

'Go up the track there—the farmhouse in the trees.'

Whatever it was it had frightened the man. Ruth listened to his wheezing breath and wondered if there might be more than one person in danger.

They were hurried through the farm living room and up narrow stairs. 'My wife's visiting her sister and I didn't know what to do,' the man gasped. 'I saw your car go up the valley and I knew it was a doctor's and. . .'

They entered a bedroom. Ruth had a momentary impression of bright curtains and cheerful wallpaper, of posters pinned on the walls and two giant teddies. Then she felt rather than heard Micah say, 'Oh, God.'

'What happened?' she asked the father quietly.

'She was up and talking an hour ago, but then she said she had a bad headache. I told her to get a drink and go to bed to rest. I came up to see her just now and. . . Is she going to be all right?'

'I'm afraid she's seriously ill. Now, phone for an ambulance, tell them it's urgent and that she must have oxygen.'

Ruth had already pulled down the bedclothes and was feeling the little girl's neck and back. She stepped back to let Micah do the same. The stiffness was unmistakable. They both knew what was wrong, but he said it. 'Meningitis.'

She nodded. 'I think so.'

'How much liquid penicillin have you got?'

'Plenty. I suppose you've got the same.' Because they spent so much time in the country, often well away from the ambulance services, all the practice members carried a well-stocked bag for emergencies.

She watched as Micah rubbed the girl's arm with surgical spirit then took a disposable syringe and jabbed it into the penicillin phial.

'What dose are you giving her?' she asked with alarm as the liquid filled the syringe.

'It's got to be a massive one. It's the kid's only chance.'

'But that dose could kill her!'

'You know she's as good as dead already. This gives her a fighting chance.'

'I suppose so,' Ruth said reluctantly. Medicine wasn't always an exact science and in this case it was difficult to decide whether he was being reckless or she was being over-cautious.

'Besides,' he went on, 'it's not just her life we're trying to save. Too small a dose and she could survive but be brain-damaged.'

Ruth shuddered. 'Right. Inject her.'

He looked for a vein. It wasn't easy; the girl's system had shut down and Ruth sighed with relief when eventually Micah managed to draw blood back in the syringe.

There was no change in the girl's condition after the injection. Both knew that the hardest part came now—the waiting. Micah slipped out to talk to the father and to see when the ambulance was expected.

Micah told the father to telephone his wife and to
arrange for his stock to be looked after. The ambulance
arrived shortly afterwards and Ruth rode in it with the
girl and her father. Micah went back to the surgery in
the Range Rover.

Micah was taking evening surgery when Ruth arrived
back at the practice, so she contented herself with
telephoning him in between patients and telling him
that the prognosis on the girl was hopeful.

'That's good news. Can we have a couple of
words later?'

'Look forward to it.' She rang off.

There was only the two of them drinking tea afterwards and between them was the intimacy that came
to people who had had to cope with an emergency
together.

First he asked after the girl's progress and she was
able to tell him that things seemed fine. He nodded
with pleasure and then said, 'The girl wasn't one of
our patients. I've asked Mary to see to the paperwork
so we can claim for the work.'

Ruth frowned. She knew she wasn't the best person
in the practice when it came to form-filling; she wanted
to be a doctor, not a clerk. But Micah's speed seemed
a bit insensitive.

He obviously felt her slight disapproval. With a smile
he said, 'I know what you're thinking. But if there's
paperwork to be done it should be done at once. Ultimately it's more efficient.'

'I suppose you're right.'

'And now you know why I want to be a GP. Didn't

you get some—well, satisfaction out of this afternoon?'

'Yes I did,' she agreed, 'but I don't want that kind of emergency too often.' She sipped her tea for a moment and then went on, 'Micah, did we really gamble with that girl's life?'

'I don't think "gamble" is the right word,' he said quietly.

'If I'd been on my own I wouldn't have given that large dose.'

It pleased her that he didn't make reassuring noises or say that she was right. After a moment he said, 'All life is a gamble. Every decision is a chance taken.'

Ruth said, 'At times you sound just like my late husband.'

There was a long pause. Then he said gently, 'Am I to take that as a compliment? Because I would like to.'

As if talking to herself she said, 'I loved him and we were happy together even if it was in a breathless sort of way. But I don't think I'll ever forgive him for dying. . . He. . .'

The door opened. 'If there's tea left I'll have some,' Martin declared.

Micah lifted the pot and waved it. 'Come and join us,' he said.


If she was going to the ball, Ruth decided, she would do the job properly. She would spend some money on herself, on a new dress. When she looked at her bank balance she was surprised at how much there was in her current account. There was easily enough to buy a new car. For a moment she wondered if indeed she was too cautious, if she should use her money while she was young and could appreciate it. She decided to spend a little.

Bannick wasn't suitable. On the Saturday afternoon of the ball she drove forty miles to Kenton, the nearest biggish town. Then she started a tour of the fashionable shops and boutiques.

When she first saw the white dress she laughed and thought, No. But throughout the next hour, no matter what she tried on, that dress remained in her mind. She went back to the tiny boutique and tried it on. It fitted perfectly. But in no way was it the dress that a respectable woman doctor should wear to a ball. 'I'll take it,' she said.

Then there were shoes, a handbag and new underwear to buy. Finally she made a trip to the best hairdresser's, where she had her long hair carefully styled. Feeling the satisfaction of having done something slightly extravagant, she went back home. For the rest of the day, until Micah came for her, she'd pamper herself, she decided.

He tapped on the door a minute before he'd said he'd arrive. Feeling both shy and excited, she opened it. She realised that for once the normally urbane Micah was lost for words.

'Ruth. . .you look wonderful,' he uttered eventually.

'Do come in,' she invited. 'I decided to spoil myself and bought a new dress.' Stepping back into her living room, she made a graceful pirouette. 'Do you like it?'

'With you as partner I'll be the most envied man at the ball,' he said. She felt a rush of pleasure at his obviously sincere words.

It was a dress that only a young and confident woman

could wear. The top was plain white silk, cut deep at the front and supported by two thin straps. There was no back. The long skirt was in flowing crêpe silk, split to the thigh and semi-transparent. Her boldness only went so far, though: she'd bought a pair of sensible white briefs too.

She knew that all eyes would be on her but for once she didn't care. Perhaps she'd been the sensible Dr Francis for too long. 'Would you like a sherry?' she asked.

As she poured he walked round her living room. There hadn't been many men in the room through the years and it was Micah's first visit. His proximity in her room, her territory, made her feel oddly excited.

She had always thought that the classic dinner jacket was one of the most flattering male outfits. Micah's suit fitted perfectly, subtly emphasising his well-built body. She could see the long muscles of his thighs and his powerful shoulders. From the subtle sheen on the material she guessed that the suit was made of mohair; the shirt was certainly made of heavy silk. Once again he was expensively dressed.

He stooped to look at her collection of tapes and CDs, neatly arranged by her music centre. 'I'm going to work out your character from your tapes,' he said, 'just like you tried to do with me.'

'They're very similar to yours,' she said. 'We have similar tastes.'

He shook his head. 'Only so far. Where I've got Sinatra you've got the "Messiah" and Mozart's "Requiem Mass".'

'I'm a very serious girl.'

He turned to look at her assessingly. 'I wonder. . .'

Next he stepped over to her bookshelf, a built-in unit that covered much of one wall. 'Books should be more revealing,' he said, scanning the titles. 'All your medical textbooks; I've got most of them myself. Four published during the past year and they're all read and annotated—you're going to keep up to date. Books for pleasure. . .Jane Austen; I might have guessed. But love poems and all of Tolkien. . . Who'd have thought you had a keen fantasy life, Ruth?'

'Here's your sherry,' she said, deciding that some of his observations were a little too shrewd.

He accepted the glass and moved to the fireplace. 'Is this your husband?' he asked, looking at the portrait.

For a moment the disloyal thought flashed across her mind that she should have moved it. 'Yes, that's Matt,' she said.

'He was an attractive man,' Micah said.

The word 'was' seemed to have a finality about it. 'He's been dead six years now,' she said.

They were now standing facing each other. 'I like your cottage,' he said. 'It's a home, not just a place to live. The Bell's all right but I really need somewhere of my own.'

'We'll have a quick guided tour, then,' she said, seizing the chance of doing something that didn't involve her having to stand and face him. 'Come and look at my patio.' She showed him the tiny garden with herbs in pots, the equally small kitchen extension. 'Bathroom and two bedrooms upstairs,' she finished. She didn't want him to look in her room, to see the double bed with the rose-coloured quilt, the essentially feminine clutter on her dressing table.

'I like it,' he said again. 'I could be very happy somewhere like this.'

There was silence as she contemplated the images that this statement brought up. She didn't know what to say. Then there was a knock on the door.

'Ruthie? It's Albert. I've brought you a bit of stuff from the allotment.'

'Come in, Albert,' she shouted, and grinned at Micah. 'Albert's a neighbour,' she explained.

'Ah.' He managed to convey much meaning in a single syllable.

Albert, the sixty-year-old farm worker from across the road, managed to shuffle in. He was hampered by three cabbages and a paper bag full of strawberries. 'Brought you these,' he explained, dumping his groceries on the settee. 'And Mavis says can she have a couple of those backache pills; she felt they did her good.'

'No trouble, Albert. But if she's really off I want to see her some time next week in the surgery. You tell her.'

During this exchange Albert had carefully avoided commenting on her or Micah's dress, but she knew he was desperate to know what the occasion was. 'We're going to a dance with the other doctors, Albert,' she said. 'This is Dr North, who's staying with us for a few months.'

'Pleased to meet you, Doctor,' said Albert. 'I'll be off now, Ruthie.'

She escorted him to the door and shut it firmly. 'A good gossip is a tonic,' she told Micah as she picked up the cabbages. 'It's part of my doctor's duties to provide stories for the neighbours.'

'I'm learning,' he said. 'Country practices are different from London ones. Would you like to walk down the street on my arm dressed like that?'

'Certainly not! I've got to live here.'

'It could provide material for an article on a new disease—tonic overdose, an investigation into the effects of too much gossip.'

'I think we'd better go,' she said.

The Range Rover was parked outside and when its door was open they were shielded from the gazes of the curious. 'This car is meant for men in wellies, not ladies in high heels,' he murmured. 'Let me help you in.'

Firm hands encircled her waist and lifted her. She liked it far more than she should have so when she was seated she said ungraciously, 'I could have managed, you know.'

'I'm sure you could,' he murmured, 'but I did enjoy it.'

Before she could answer he was striding round to the driver's seat.

The weather in Bannick tended to be erratic but today they were fortunate. As they drove through the well-loved countryside in the late afternoon sun Ruth thought she'd never seen it so beautiful. A sense of anticipation seized her; she was looking forward to this evening more than she'd looked forward to anything for years.

'You've organised everything so far,' she said, 'so I felt I had to do my bit. I've arranged for someone to come and pick us up. You don't need to worry about drinking and driving.'

'Now that's thoughtful of you. I don't drink much—but it'll be good not to have to count the glasses.'

'We doctors have to set an example,' she said mock-primly.

He took her seriously. 'A lot of my colleagues in London drank far too much. Medicine is getting to be one of the risk professions for alcoholism.'

'I know.' She paused for a moment. 'Do you miss living in London?'

He shook his head decisively. 'Not a bit. I did everything I wanted to do in London. There are too many people there with an eye to making a quick profit. It's too competitive, too many people with ulcers.'

He paused, and Ruth noted the smile of contentment as his eyes wandered over the sunlit scene around them. 'I've got no family,' he said. 'I envy you your roots. I want to live somewhere like this—somewhere beautiful, somewhere stable. I want to raise a family here.'

Ruth said nothing. She wondered what he'd meant when he'd said he'd done everything he wanted to do in London but she didn't ask him.

They drove into the grounds of Lord Dallan's castle and an efficient security guard took their ticket and directed them to a parking place. Then they walked through the stepped gardens and up to the front entrance. They met more than a few people that Ruth knew, and she took delight first in observing their amazement at her dress and then at Micah. She introduced him simply as 'the practice trainee'.

'You're enjoying this,' he growled after the fourth

introduction. 'You make me sound like a spotty twenty-three-year-old.'

'Of course. If I'm going to be the subject of gossip I want it to be juicy.'

'I shall do my bit to make the gossip about us unbelievably juicy.'

'I'm shivering in anticipation,' she said, knowing she was only half joking.

Once through the imposing front door they were shown to a table for two, as promised, in the grand banqueting hall. She blinked at the size of the champagne bottle that rested in a silver ice bowl. 'It's called a nebuchadnezzar,' Micah explained. 'I ordered it from London. What we don't drink now we can take into the dance later to share with the others.'

He raised his eyebrows when she said, 'If there's any left.'

There was a loud pop as the waiter slid off the cork. He leaned over to fill her glass, and she tasted. 'I like it,' she said.

The meal was good but she didn't pay much attention to it. She wanted to enjoy herself, and was more interested in her surroundings and in her companion. Micah responded to her mood and they had a cheerful light-hearted conversation. As he filled her glass for the second time she wondered how long it had been since she had let herself enjoy herself so thoroughly. You'll get to be an old maid, she thought with a tiny twinge of panic.

When the dinner was over they took coffee on the terrace and enjoyed the distant view of grey mountains, and the scent of flowers from the gardens below. It was soon time to drift to the marquee where the dance was to be held and meet the others.

She got on well with Enid, Harry's wife, and Sue, Martin's wife. Micah was introduced and welcomed straight away. Sue caught Ruth's eye with a speculative wink that made her blush.

'This is very pleasant,' said Micah, indicating their white-clothed table with its posies of flowers. A waiter had brought their nebuchadnezzar, fortunately with plenty still in, and was pouring them all a drink.

'Just don't fall ill,' Harry warned. 'Fifteen years ago someone did—the MC asked that if there was a doctor in the house would he come behind the stage. The only person to turn up was a cook with a first aid certificate. All the doctors reckoned it was their turn to have a rest.'

In the midst of the general laughter the band started to play.

Ruth wasn't surprised to find that Micah was an excellent dancer. She'd noticed his athlete's way of moving, his sensitivity to music. Their bodies seemed to fit together perfectly, with none of the hesitations she'd felt with other partners. She gave herself up to the moment, conscious of nothing but her joy in the movement and the arms of her partner around her.

It was necessary, of course, to dance with both Harry and Martin. 'Enjoying yourself?' Harry asked, cheerfully kicking her feet out of the way so that he could negotiate a corner.

'I really am; it's bliss,' she confessed dreamily.

'It's good to see you enjoying yourself, Ruth. Sometimes I think. . .you take yourself and your work too seriously.'

'Tonight, Harry, work is a four-letter word.'

He squeezed her hand and said nothing.

It was getting slightly warm in the marquee so Micah asked if she'd like a walk in the garden, where several other couples were doing the same. They walked out into the early dusk. Overhead a bat skittered past.

'The bat's the Chinese emblem of happiness,' he told her.

'All part of the service,' she replied. She didn't object when he took hold of her hand.

The temperature was perfect. They strolled at random, passing heavily scented rose beds and mossy statues. The sound of other people's voices died away; there was only the distant throb of the band. The night felt like magic.

She knew what was happening when he stopped by a carefully cut yew alcove and gently pulled her into the shade. For a moment they faced each other, his hands on her arms. Then he drew her towards him.

It was a gentle kiss at first. He held her tentatively, as a man might hold a wild bird. His lips brushed her cheek before settling on her own half-parted mouth. She was almost surprised when her initial wariness slowly ebbed away. It felt right to be here in his arms, smelling the combination of expensive cologne and the warm maleness of his body.

'I don't kiss just anybody,' she said breathlessly, moving away a little before he could know just what effect he was having on her.

'I hope I'm not just anybody,' he whispered, urging her towards him again, 'and I've wanted to kiss you ever since you shouted at me in the surgery.'

'I thought you had a gorgeous voice,' she confessed,

and then thought how trite that sounded. 'And I liked you,' she added.

He kissed her again and this time she reacted to his growing passion, her mouth opening under his exciting onslaught. 'Ruth,' he muttered, his hands trailing fire across her naked back. 'Ruth, I. . .'

All her senses seemed doubly alive. Her fingers thrilled to the crispness of his hair, the fragrance of flowers mingled with the scent of his maleness. She could taste his lips, hear. . . She could hear the distant dance music, the sound of some night bird and close at hand the crunch of gravel. Someone was walking towards them.

She sensed his reluctance but he made no move to stop her as she stepped back from him. 'Doctor, you're thinking of your reputation again,' he whispered.

'And yours,' she whispered back. 'You have to practise in this town, too.'

He stepped out of their little bower and took her arm as they set off back towards the marquee. He nudged her gently and said softly, 'D'you think it's something in the air?'

Ahead of them was the silhouette of another couple, also embracing. Micah coughed to warn of their approach and the couple parted and fled.

'That was the nicest thing that's happened to me since I came to Bannick,' he said gently. When she made no reply he went on, 'I think you're supposed to say something nice to me now.'

'I'm frightened, Micah,' she confessed. 'Not of you but of me.'

He squeezed her arm. 'We've got all the time in the world.'

But Ruth felt as if she was being forced to think of things she had long decided would never be any business of hers again.

Back at their table they found that supper was being served. It wasn't too long since dinner but she found herself unaccountably hungry and readily tucked into the smoked salmon and salad. 'The open air obviously gave you an appetite,' Micah murmured.

She murmured back, 'Something did,' and then marvelled at her own brazenness. What was happening to her?

Harry was craning his neck to look around. He exclaimed, 'That's a bit of a surprise! Look, it's Lord Dallan.'

'I thought he wasn't coming!' Ruth looked up, startled at Micah's harsh tone. He looked wary, and had half risen from his seat. She didn't know what was worrying him.

'He doesn't usually come,' Harry said. 'Claims business in London keeps him down there. But he's quite a nice chap; I've met him before.'

Ruth watched Micah uneasily. His expression was now bland, a half-smile on his face, but she felt that some part of him had withdrawn from them. He was calculating, but what she didn't know.

Lord Dallan, white-haired but militarily erect, was visiting every table. Ruth appreciated his social skills; he showed no sign of fatigue and remembered everyone's name and job.

Now it was their turn. 'Harry, so glad you could come.'

Harry shook hands and then introduced the rest of

the table. Lord Dallan had an urbane word for each, and then Harry said, 'And this is Dr Micah North. He's working with us for a while.'

'Dr North.' The already standing Micah leaned forward to take the proffered hand. Then Ruth noticed Lord Dallan's shrewd eyes suddenly register something. 'Micah North—that's an unusual name. Didn't you work in the City for Clay Hutchinson Talbot?'

Only Ruth was aware of the icy calm that had descended on Micah. 'Yes. I worked for them for some years.'

'You were their ace foreign exchange and currency man. They offered you a fortune to stay—couldn't work out why you left.'

'I left to train as a doctor.'

'I see,' Lord Dallan said slowly, though it was obvious that he did not. 'Do I have to register with your practice to get your financial advice? Perhaps we could have a chat some time?'

Everyone on the table now knew that something was amiss. Tight-lipped, Micah said, 'We can offer you medical advice. But I no longer have any dealings with the market.'

'Pity,' Lord Dallan said bluntly, then he realised he'd been rude. 'Well, good luck in your new career, Dr North. I'll be in touch.' Reluctantly he moved to the next table.

Their table was quiet and Ruth was still trying to come to terms with what she'd heard. She just didn't understand the implications of what had been said. She knew that Micah wasn't pleased. And she had a sick feeling that things were going to get worse.

It was Martin's wife, Sue, who spoke first. She was

an ex-nurse and Ruth had always liked her forthright manner. 'Micah, there's something you haven't told us. We all know you're a good doctor but you've got to tell us what it is. We all have to know and trust each other.'

Ruth's heart was hammering. She didn't know why she was panicking, but she felt that this revelation was going to change things.

Micah glanced at her ruefully. 'It's nothing really discreditable,' he said. 'But I wanted to make my way just as a doctor and I was afraid that this would alter your perception of me. I started work in the City as an office boy and worked my way up. Eventually I became the firm's number one foreign exchange dealer—paid on commission.' He sighed and looked round the table. 'I made ridiculous amounts of money. In fact I'm a millionaire five or six times over.'

'Is that all?' Harry asked airily.

# CHAPTER FOUR

RUTH didn't know what to think. Of all the possible revelations about Micah, of all the dark secrets that could have been unveiled, this was one she'd never even considered.

She looked at him, handsome in his dinner jacket and apparently imperturbable. He was determined to bend the conversation back to where it had been before, by a sheer effort of will. If he could do it, then she could show the same strength.

'We don't want Lord Dallan as a patient anyway,' he said with a smile. 'Looks like the kind of man who calls you out in the middle of the night for no good reason.'

Martin chimed in, 'A definite gout type. Far too much port and Stilton. We'd never get him on a diet.'

Gloomily Harry pushed his plate away. 'I was enjoying my bit of cheese till you spoke, Martin. Micah, you've given us all a bit of a shock. But it's certainly nothing discreditable, and now I think we should talk about something else. This night's too special to talk about money.'

'I agree. Let me fill our glasses.' Micah plucked the champagne from the ice bucket. As he leaned over the table, bottle in hand, Ruth gazed into his grey-green eyes. She knew how easily he could mask his feelings. But she felt there was an appeal there that she could not ignore.

Raising her glass to her lips, she said, 'I could get to like this, Micah. It's better than halves of shandy.'

'It's also less caloric. The harm lemonade can do is tremendous.'

There was a gentle laugh at this sally. Then the band struck up again and Harry and Martin led their wives onto the floor.

Alone with Micah, Ruth didn't know what to say. Her gaze drifted round the marquee but scarcely registered the slowly twisting figures against the red and white swathes of material lining the tent. He would have to make the first move.

'Would you like to dance, Ruth?'

She smiled her assent. 'Love to.' They stepped onto the floor and she gave herself up to the music. But the sense of togetherness she had felt when they'd danced before had somehow gone. They moved as fluidly, but she could tell by his assessing gaze and the tightness of his arm around her waist that he was worried.

He swept her expertly round a corner and she said playfully, 'You're about to say something serious and depressing and I don't want you to.'

'You're getting to know me well, Ruth.'

'We've just found out that I don't know you well at all.' He had the grace to look uncomfortable. She went on, 'So far this evening has been magic and I don't think I'll ever forget it. So don't say anything to spoil it.'

After a pause he said, 'The evening's not over yet and the magic could carry on.'

She shook her head. 'All magic ends. In every fairy story there's a time limit and a price to pay.'

'There's also a happy ending,' he suggested.

'That depends on the fairy story.'

Before he could reply the dance ended. They looked silently at each other for a moment and then he escorted her back to their table.

There was a roll on the drums and the MC, a local solicitor, walked to the microphone. Time for the speeches—which were usually kept mercifully short.

The MC thanked Lord Dallan for the use of his home—'so nice to see him in person this year'—and thanked them all for coming. More money than ever had been raised this year. The local hospital would benefit by it and so, indirectly, would all the doctors present. As the laughter died down at this little joke, he said that the only thing left was the raffle draw.

'I love raffles,' Enid said. 'But I've never ever won.' They all stared at the strips of coloured tickets they'd bought earlier.

The prizes were generous, donated by businesses in Bannick itself. The number was called and the third prize collected—announced as a Ministry pamphlet on the dangers of cholesterol and overeating, with a giant food hamper and box of chocolates to go with it. The second prize was a pamphlet on alcohol abuse—with a case of vintage Burgundy. The first prize went to the owner of pink ticket number 45251.

'Pink, number 45251,' shouted the MC. 'The prize is a circular on how to obtain medical attention when abroad. And to go with it Bannick Travel Agency has given us a romantic weekend for two in Paris, to be taken at any time in the next six months. Somebody must have the ticket.'

Ruth smiled as people around looked at their tickets

afresh, as if staring might change the numbers. 'Check your tickets, Ruth,' Enid commanded.

Ruth shook her head. 'Like you, I never win.'

Enid reached over for Ruth's tickets. 'Pink 45251,' she squeaked. 'Ruth, you've won!'

People on the surrounding tables heard Enid's cry and began to clap. Horrified, Ruth grasped the proffered slip of paper. Yes. She *had* won.

'Don't keep him waiting, Ruth,' Micah advised with a smile, and moved round to ease back her chair.

'Come with me,' she whispered urgently to him as she stood.

'To collect a romantic Holiday for two in Paris? What would that do for your reputation?'

Alarmed at the very idea, she set off at once across the floor. The MC handed her an envelope and said into the microphone, 'A condition of this prize is that the winner tells us next year just how she got on.'

The crowd roared and Ruth blushed and giggled as she walked back to her place. It was a good thing she was among friends, she thought.

Her friends seemed more pleased about the prize than Ruth did. They opened the envelope and looked eagerly at the hotel address and details of the flight.

'It's no good to me,' Ruth said. 'It's nice winning but I've got no one to be romantic in Paris with. Which of you two old married couples wants a second honeymoon?'

Sue grabbed the envelope and pushed it firmly into Ruth's bag. 'It's for you,' she said. 'You won it. Let's have no more of your nonsense.'

Ruth didn't argue. She caught a glimpse of Micah

smiling at her; as so often his face was an amiable mask.

People started leaving the ball quite early. Many of the doctors there had travelled some distance and more than a few of them would be working the next day. Martin had family commitments and Harry went with him, so Ruth suggested that she and Micah leave too. He agreed. She made a phone call and they went to stand on the steps at the front of the hall. Quite a few other couples had decided to leave their cars and were there waiting for taxis.

'Around here, if you're a doctor and you're caught drunk driving then you've had it,' Ruth said. 'The magistrates will make an example of you.'

He nodded. 'Good. If you hadn't arranged transport I would have limited myself to just two glasses—and that would have been terrible.'

'I did like the champagne,' she agreed.

'I thought the whole evening was wonderful.'

She didn't reply and a minute later Albert Day pulled up in a large and ancient Vauxhall.

Micah looked at it with some doubt. 'Will we be quite safe in that?' he asked.

'Albert's son is a motor mechanic,' Ruth told him. 'That car is as sound as the day it was first delivered.'

'Which was about twenty-five years ago,' he muttered, but smiled anyway.

'I use Albert a lot,' she told him. 'It's one of those unofficial country arrangements that work quite well.'

'Would he bring me back here tomorrow to pick up my car?'

She assured him that Albert would be delighted.

They sat in the back of Albert's car, sinking deep into the extra cushions he had supplied. Albert didn't drive fast. He had to concentrate on his gossip. 'Have a good time, then, Ruth?'

'Super, Albert. We didn't want to leave. But there'll be problems tomorrow. Doctoring's like farming—it never stops.'

'That's true. Did you hear. . .?' Albert started on a long story she realised he'd told her before. Things didn't change.

In the darkness Micah's hand covered hers and squeezed it gently. She squeezed it back, then pushed it equally gently away. She didn't want Albert gossiping. Micah seemed to sense this and joined in the general talk.

'Are you both going back to yours, Ruth?' Albert asked suddenly.

'No. Can you drop Dr North off at the Bell Hotel first?'

'Certainly can.'

'But Ruth—' Micah began, but she interrupted him.

'I know you want to see me safely home but that would mean Albert having to drive all the way back to Bannick.'

'I suppose it makes sense,' he sighed, and she could feel the frustration in his voice. She smiled wryly.

The car continued its dignified progress.

'Are you on call tomorrow?' Micah asked suddenly.

'No. I take it you are?'

'Not exactly. Apparently Bannick Rugby Club is playing a friendly game out of season—and since it's a friendly game they think there might be injuries. I've been asked if I'll come and stand by. There's no fee but I have the freedom of the hospitality room. That means as many pies and as much beer as I can consume.'

Ruth chuckled. 'I told you country medicine was different.'

'I'd rather play than be doctor but I'm quite looking forward to it. Do you take an interest in the game?'

In a matter-of-fact tone she said, 'My husband played for Bannick. In fact the first time I ever met him he was being carried off a rugby field.'

'I'm sorry,' he said gently.

'It doesn't matter. I can see the game's attraction—to men.'

He touched her hand again but didn't attempt to hold it.

The car drew up outside a portico and Albert switched on the interior light. 'The Bell Hotel,' he said unnecessarily, and turned to look at his two passengers.

Ruth had expected this and grinned sardonically at Micah's obvious frustration. 'Don't worry about my getting home,' she said quickly. 'I'm among friends. Thanks for a wonderful evening, Micah. I thoroughly enjoyed it.'

'I enjoyed it too,' he said. 'I. . .'

She stretched out her hand for him to shake. 'I'm ready for bed,' she said. 'Goodnight, Micah.'

She could see the emotions warring in his face. There was irritation and frustration but also a realisation of the humour in the situation. His hand hadn't yet released hers and his thumb gently stroked the soft flesh of her palm. 'Next time will be different,' he whispered, and she didn't know if it was a threat or a promise.

He stepped out of the car, looked round, and said, 'I feel restless. I think I'll go for a walk before I go to bed. Goodnight.'

As Albert drove away she turned to look at the solitary figure, dressed in black and white, in the middle of the Georgian square. There was confidence and power in the angle of his shoulders, the set of his neck as he strolled across the cobbles. Ruth felt a twinge of anxiety. Should she play with such a man?

Albert dropped her off at home after detailing all of his and his family's ailments. She entered her own little house with a slight sigh of relief. It had been a full day and she needed time to herself.

Before stepping out of it, she inspected herself in her wonderful new dress. She had to admit that she looked good. All through the evening at the ball she'd been conscious of a hum of interest, from both men and women. Most of them knew her; none had ever seen her dressed like this. She rather liked it.

She hung up the dress, bathed, creamed her face, put on her dressing gown and went to make herself a cup of bedtime cocoa. The simple tasks gave her something to do, something to stop her thinking. Tomorrow would be soon enough to grapple with her new discoveries.

As she passed the fireplace her unfocused eyes drifted over the picture of Matt. She stopped to pick it up. Once, she realised, she would never pass this picture without looking and, just for a moment, grieving. But she hadn't done that for a while now. The face looking at her was from the past. With a feeling of relief she realised what had happened. She had loved Matt, mourned him fiercely when he died, even felt anger at him for leaving her. But now he had gone. She touched her lips to the cold glass. Goodbye, Matt, she thought.

Sitting in bed clutching her cocoa, she remembered something. In her handbag was the envelope with the details of her romantic weekend for two in Paris. She looked at the address—she hadn't been to Paris since a school trip many years ago. She thought it would be nice to go.

It had been a gorgeous evening. She liked the company of her friends and their wives, the food, the music, the setting. . . Who was she trying to kid? She'd been kissed in the garden by Micah and had responded in a way that had both exhilarated and frightened her. She hadn't felt this way in years. It was as if a spring had opened in her heart.

But Micah was rich, and she found that unsettling. Ruefully, she smiled. She couldn't think of many women who would be upset at discovering that a man who was interested in them was madly wealthy. She herself cared little for money.

A faint uneasiness crept over her. Once she'd attended a lecture to do with the medical problems of battered wives. The lecturer had told them that a common syndrome was for a woman somehow to rid herself of one vicious male—and promptly take up with another. Ruth shivered. In character Matt and Micah were vastly different. But they also had something in common. She couldn't go through that again.

Surprisingly she slept well, but woke early the next morning. It was one of those rare days in early summer when she wouldn't have wanted to be anywhere else in the world but Bannick. She made her early-morning coffee and stepped into the garden. The air was like the champagne she'd drunk last night, with a slight breeze bringing the scent of the moors and the distant calling of birds.

She read the Sunday papers and wandered round the garden, washing, weeding, doing odd household jobs. For a while she was happy just to be, not to think. Thinking she'd do later.

At lunchtime the telephone rang. Deliberately she let it; her answering machine would take any important message. After five minutes she walked inside and turned on the tape.

'Hi,' said the machine, 'it's Micah.'

Her finger stabbed down on the pause button. She had not thought that that humorous dark brown voice could cause such immediate turmoil. But it had. Telling herself not to be so foolish, she lifted her finger. His voice was pleasant and relaxed, without that anxiety that affected people having to concentrate on their message.

He went on, 'I hope you enjoyed last night. I phoned to say how much I did. Apart from that, I've just arrived at the Rec. The sun's shining and as well as rugby there are two ladies' hockey teams playing. They look much more fearsome than the men. If you wanted to be team doctor I think there might be work for you. I'll be on the touchline from three o'clock onwards. We could share a meat pie afterwards?'

Her lips twitched into a smile. It was the perfect invitation, friendly and non-threatening. She'd been wondering about how they'd next meet; this would be ideal.

First from her wardrobe she took a summer dress
in a pastel pink colour that went beautifully with her
dark hair. Then she sighed and returned it. She was
going as a doctor. Trousers and a sweater would be
far more practical.

The bit of ground known as the Rec—short for rec-
reation ground—was on the outskirts of Bannick.
Today it was busy. She counted no less than four different matches, and no end of spectators thronged the
various pitches.

She parked and walked over to the one rugby match.
Micah was easy to spot among the other spectators;
no one else was so broad-shouldered, so tall. He was
dressed today in dark trousers and a blue blazer, and
she could just see the gold badge of some club on the
breast pocket. She approached him from the side and
when she called his name and he turned her heart
leaped.

'Ruth, how nice to see you. I left a message but I
thought you might be out all day.'

To conceal her turbulent emotions she took refuge
in a professional coolness. 'I was going to go for a walk.
But when you said so many were playing I thought you
might need an extra doctor.'

A lifted eyebrow showed that he recognised this
fiction for what it was. 'Let's hope we're not needed.
Anyway, I'm enjoying watching. Bannick here seem
quite a good team. I've been offered a trial for next
season.'

'You're not going to accept, are you?' Her concern
showed in the hastiness of her question.

He laughed and stroked his nose. 'I've broken this
twice. The second time the ENT consultant insisted

on teaching me as well as treating me. You've no idea how unfascinating a deviated septum is when you're the patient. I decided to retire from rugby.'

' "A game for louts played by gentlemen",' she said, quoting one of her husband's favourite maxims. 'You're well out of it.'

'Anyway, my contract here is only for a year.'

She had forgotten that. The thought of Micah North leaving didn't please her.

As he took her arm and urged her down the touchline she took refuge in a pretence of cool concern. 'Did you collect your car this morning?'

'Indeed I did. Had a long talk with Albert. Apparently he's known you since you were a child.'

She winced and said, 'Albert loves a good story. Whether it's true or not isn't important.'

'So you didn't fall into the stream with the missing apples?'

'Yes, I did. But I didn't know Albert's son had stolen them.'

'Quite,' he said smugly.

It all seemed a bit unfair to Ruth. She didn't know anything discreditable about his childhood.

'I really enjoyed last night,' he said. 'I thought you looked wonderful and I saw a lot of people eyeing your dress. I think you surprised them.'

'I surprised myself,' she said frankly. 'Just for once I wanted to be something more than the conventional small-town doctor.'

'Just for once?' he queried.

She nodded firmly. 'Just for once. Now I'm back where I'm happy.'

She might have guessed that he wouldn't hesitate

but that he'd meet any problem head-on. After a pause he said, 'I enjoy your company, Ruth. Last night I thought we were moving towards—well, an under-standing. Then you found out something about me that I'd kept from you. Did you feel let down—deceived?'

Answering was difficult. She felt definitely that something had changed—and for the worse. But she couldn't decide what. 'I've never met a multimillionaire before,' she said. 'It changes a lot. You can't expect me to treat you just as our trainee.'

'I was hoping you would. I'm still a doctor learning his trade.'

This, she decided, was the heart of the problem. 'So tell me why you want to be a country GP. You could have been anything. You don't even need ever to work again if you don't want. Why this job?'

'Do you do it just for money?' he asked quietly.

She shook her head. 'No. I'm a doctor here because I love it.'

'That's what I want. I'm a romantic, really. I want to put down roots, to belong to a community. In London I had good friends but they still competed with me. It was life on the edge all the time. Thrilling—but not very peaceful.'

'But why medicine?'

'My parents died when I was young and I was brought up by Great-Aunt Molly. She suffered from a variety of complaints—arthritis, congested lungs— the result, I suppose, of a long, hard life in poor accom-modation. Towards the end of her life, because of new drugs and treatments, things got easier. Her GP took obvious delight in treating her. And I thought, That's for me. But first I had to make money.'

Gently, she asked, 'How did your parents die when you were so young?'

'They were killed by terrorists while they were teaching in the bush in Africa. There was some kind of insurrection and they were told it was dangerous. They sent me to a mission fifty miles away but they stayed on.'

He paused for a moment and she could tell that he wasn't used to talking about himself. After a moment he went on, 'So I was sent back to England to my only relative and she devoted the rest of her life to looking after me.'

'So your great-aunt never knew you'd become a doctor?'

He shook his head. 'She knew it was my ambition and she desperately wanted me to stay on at school to take A levels. But I wanted to give something back. So I got a job in the City and just for a while before she died I was able to give her a few of the things she'd missed. That pleased me. The A levels I took one at a time at night school and by correspondence.'

'You've had a hard life,' Ruth said thoughtfully.

'No. I've enjoyed it.'

It slipped out before she could stop it. 'You never got married—no girlfriends?'

He laughed. 'Girlfriends of course. And I nearly got engaged once. Bit of a joke really—I'll tell you about it when I know you better.'

They paced on in silence, Ruth absorbed by what she had heard. It all made sense. But she was uneasy. Having lived life on the edge, could he ever settle down to real tranquillity? She sensed in him that urge to make snap decisions, to gamble with life, that had been so obvious a part of her dead husband's make-up. And she couldn't live with that again.

'I don't like shocks, sudden desperate decisions,' she said. 'They unsettle me.'

'Life isn't a settled business.'

Medicine had taught her that that was true. But she had to at least try to control it.

It was sad, but she couldn't help thinking about the fact that he was rich. Somehow it came between them. 'What's happened to your money now?'

He shrugged. 'I made the decision to give up dealing and start my medical course. The money's looked after by a stockbroker friend. All I do is receive the interest.'

There was a roar from the crowd and they turned to see that Bannick had scored. As they joined in the clapping Micah grinned at her. 'We really should be supporting the home team, you know. Too much serious conversation on a Sunday is bad for one.'

'It might be bad for you, but I'm a serious girl.' They watched as the losing team kicked off and then she said, 'There's one more question. You're rich, good-looking, clever. Why pick on me? Is it just because I'm handy?'

'That question doesn't flatter you or me, Ruth.'

'Give me an answer anyway.'

He paused and then said, 'I find you. . .'

He had been right when he'd phoned earlier. The accident happened in a ladies' hockey match. As he spoke to her, brow furrowed, they heard the thud of running footsteps behind them and a distressed girl's voice called, 'Please, are you the doctor?'

They turned to see a young girl in blue hockey kit. Even though she was upset and out of breath Ruth was amused to see that she was instantly rather impressed with Micah.

'We're both doctors,' Micah smiled. 'What's the problem?'

The girl pointed to the far hockey field. Play had obviously stopped and there was a knot of players and spectators gathered round someone on the ground.

'Evelyn got hit in the mouth by a ball. There's blood and teeth everywhere and she's ever so upset.'

'I'll bet,' Micah murmured. He dug in his pocket and brought out a bunch of keys. 'Ruth, I left a bag in my car over there. I'll go and get it if you want to go and take a look?'

'See you there.' The girl wanted her to run but Ruth wasn't going to arrive hot and panting. She jogged gently over. 'Excuse me, I'm a doctor.' It always worked, spoken loudly and with authority. The crowd parted to reveal a girl sitting on the ground, being supported and comforted by two other players. Gently Ruth eased one aside and knelt by the sobbing figure. 'See if you can find a blanket,' she said to the player she'd displaced. 'She could go into shock.'

There was blood dripping down the girl's front, apparently from a cut in her lip. The girl was trying to stem it, holding her shirt against her mouth.

For the moment Ruth ignored it. She quickly took her pulse—fast, of course, but not dangerously so. Then she peered in each eye, checking for dilation or uneven size of the pupils. So far there was no sign of concussion.

'Right, Evelyn,' she said gently. 'I'm a doctor. I know it hurts and it looks a mess but we'll soon have you sorted out. Now let me look at your mouth. Come on, move your hands away.'

Two tearful eyes stared at her, and with a sound that was half-sob, half-hiccup the girl said, 'Toot.'

Oh no, Ruth thought, but kept her expression of calmness and sympathy. She managed to move the girl's hands away. The mouth was a mess. Ruth wiped away what blood she could with a tissue taken from her pocket. The bottom lip was badly split and would probably need stitching. There appeared to be further, lesser cuts inside the mouth. But what was most distressing was the sight of an empty bloody socket. One of Evelyn's front teeth had been knocked out.

'Here, use this.' Ruth was surprised to find Micah crouched next to her, offering her a sterile pad to dab away the blood.

'Lost her front tooth,' she muttered as she looked more closely at the split lip. To her surprise Micah stood up at once.

'Quiet a minute, please,' she heard him call authoritatively, and there was instant silence. 'Now, where exactly was Evelyn standing when she got hit?'

'She was running to intercept,' a voice ventured, 'and she ran on quite a few yards before she fell over.'

'Right. Now, all of you form a line here and crawl on your hands and knees till you find a knocked-out tooth. When you do don't touch it. Shout for me.' To another player he said, 'Run to the pavilion and say the doctor wants a glass full of ice urgently.'

From the contents of Micah's bag Ruth contrived a rough dressing for Evelyn's bottom lip. Wadding together some sterile dressing, she eased it round the empty socket. Someone arrived with a blanket and she wrapped it round the still shuddering shoulders, telling Evelyn that she'd soon be safe in hospital.

From the line of searching girls came a shout. 'It's here!' Micah stooped and took an empty plastic phial from his bag. His face close to Ruth, he smiled and winked. Then he filled the phial with ice and went to drop the tooth in it.

There was someone still kneeling with Evelyn. Micah carefully pulled Ruth away. 'The sooner she gets to an emergency dental service, the better her chances of getting the tooth back in,' he said. 'Shall I take her?'

'I think I'd better,' Ruth said. 'I know the way. I'll get one of her friends to go with me. I'll take her to hospital. The facio-maxillary unit is on Tapley Road.'

As she turned to fetch her car, he whispered, 'And Ruth?'

'Yes?'

'We've got a conversation to finish. Don't forget.'

'Just let me get this girl out of here.'

There was the usual flurry of explanations, arrangements, decisions. Micah put his arm round Evelyn, raised her to her feet and half-carried her to Ruth's car. He promised to phone ahead to tell them what to expect. Two girls volunteered to go with their teammate. Then Ruth was bumping onto the road, Evelyn in the back, the precious phial in her pocket.

She was happy to hand over her charge to the efficient processes of the facio-maxillary unit. When she was sure there was nothing else she could do she drove back to the Rec. All the matches were finished, but an excited crowd in the clubroom gathered round her, asking about Evelyn.

'Evelyn should be all right,' Ruth said. 'Now it's my

turn to preach. How many of you wear a gumshield when you're playing?' Two of the team raised their hands; the rest looked sheepish.

'If Evelyn had been wearing a gumshield she wouldn't have lost a tooth,' Ruth said. 'There's a message for you all there.'

With a smile she declined the offer of a drink and went in search of Micah.

He wasn't to be found. One of the rugby team said he'd watched till the end but had then had an urgent phone call from his hotel. A little worried, Ruth phoned the Bell and identified herself as a doctor.

'I don't think it's anything medical,' the receptionist said. 'Mr North had a phone call. Could he go to Manchester urgently. He told us he wasn't likely to be back till very late. The night porter will let him in.'

Funny he didn't leave a message, Ruth thought. Of course, there were all sorts of reasons why he might have had to go to Manchester. But she couldn't get over the fact that she was a bit disappointed. And perhaps a bit troubled, too.

## CHAPTER FIVE

THE good weather carried on the next day. Ruth drove into work, enjoying the sun on the mountainsides, the smells of the countryside through her open window. Mozart played softly on her cassette player, a piece she'd last listened to with Micah. She felt calm.

She knew exactly what she was doing—something quite unusual for her. She was *not* making a decision, *not* thinking things through. Micah North had aroused turbulent feelings in her and she needed to wait, to see if they'd settle.

Occasionally over the past few years she'd been invited out by a man, for dinner or drinks. Nothing had ever come of it. None of them had remotely interested her. But Micah did. She could now feel emotions welling inside her that she'd thought long buried. But she was—frightened? There was a remorseless quality about Micah that could lead to him taking risks like Matt.

She'd give herself a week of not thinking about him. Having decided that, she caught herself feeling disappointed when she rolled into the practice car park and the red Range Rover wasn't there.

Morning surgery took its normal course. There was the odd new problem but mostly cases she could easily deal with. Then, when the morning was nearly over, Mary rang through on the intercom. 'Could you have a quick word with Nurse Mathers, Doctor?'

Celia Mathers was the practice midwife. She was vastly experienced, and currently running an antenatal clinic a hundred yards down the road in a church hall.

'Dr Francis?' Ruth could detect that the usually serene Celia was either angry or upset.

'What's the problem, Celia?'

'Gail Thompson is the problem. I know she's young and going to be an unmarried mum but I can't have her upsetting all the others. It's not fair.'

'What has she done?' Ruth asked patiently. She knew that Celia took her responsibilities very seriously.

'Well, we were halfway through the relaxation programme when Miss Gail started screaming that she was fed up and she didn't want the baby. She never asked for it and it wasn't her fault.' Nurse Mathers sniffed. 'Not her fault indeed. There's people in that class been hoping for a baby for years and it upset them.'

'Is she still there?'

'Well, she's not in my class. I whipped her out double quick and put her in the back room with a cup of tea. There's just no talking to her.'

'No medical problems at all, Celia?'

'None at all. Baby's doing fine. All it needs is another mother.'

Or a father, Ruth thought to herself, but wisely said nothing. Celia had views on unmarried parents which she was ever ready to air.

'Look, Celia, try to keep her there and I'll come over for a chat in ten minutes. I've nearly finished surgery.'

'She needs a good talking-to,' Celia said, and rang off. Ruth grinned and buzzed Mary to ask her to pull Gail Thompson's card. She suspected that this case was going to take quite some time.

Before she walked over to the church hall she snatched a cup of coffee and flicked through Gail's case notes. Like so many cases, it was as much social as medical.

Gail was just seventeen, one of three children of a family who weren't well off but who were, as the notes in front of Ruth explained, 'respectable'. The father of the child was known—Jerry Smart, another student at the local high school. He was even younger than Gail. There was no prospect of marriage and in fact Gail's mother had proudly said that they wanted nothing to do with the boy or his family. The local social worker was keeping an eye on the situation.

Ruth sighed. Another tiny local tragedy. All she could really do was ensure that Gail and her baby had the best of medical attention. She grabbed her bag and went to the church hall.

Celia was gently shepherding her soon-to-be mothers out of the hall, smiling, reassuring and telling them to call if there was any problem. When she saw Ruth she grimaced and jerked her thumb towards the door to the little back room. Not wanting to be waylaid by an anxious mum, Ruth walked rapidly across the floor.

She opened the door—and a magazine thumped into the wall by her side. 'It's all rubbish,' someone sobbed, and Ruth stepped in calmly and shut the door behind her.

'I wish you wouldn't throw things,' she said.

It didn't appear as if the magazine had been thrown at her deliberately. Gail was sitting opposite her, a pathetic, weeping child, looking far too young for motherhood. By her side was a pile of magazines and an untouched cup of tea.

'I tell you, it's all rubbish,' she cried. 'Why do they bother to print it?'

Ruth decided the matter-of-fact approach was best. 'Get on the couch, Gail,' she said, 'and let's have a look at you.'

'I'm fed up of being looked at! I've been poked and examined and I've had enough of it!'

But Gail wasn't a real rebel. Ruth looked at her and said nothing. After a minute the girl miserably stood up and shuffled over to the old examination couch.

At first Gail was uncooperative, complaining and fidgeting while Ruth took her blood pressure, listened to her heart, felt her abdomen. She knew that Celia would have done this already, but she expected the examination to have a soothing effect.

Eventually it worked. Gail's sobs slowly declined. As Celia had said, there was nothing medically wrong. 'You're in good shape,' Ruth commented. 'Now sit here quietly while I fetch you a fresh cup of tea and we'll have a little talk.'

Gail wiped her eyes. 'What's to talk about?'

'I'm hoping you'll tell me.'

Rapid mood switches weren't unusual in pregnancy. Ruth wasn't too surprised when Gail became considerably more resigned after sipping her fresh tea. 'Those articles,' she said bitterly, indicating the pile of women's magazines left by the ladies of the church. 'They're all rubbish. That's why I threw one. I didn't throw it at you,' she added anxiously.

'I know you didn't, Gail. What upset you?'

Gail fetched the offending magazine and turned to

the centre pages. 'Look at that,' she complained. How TO MAKE YOUR LOVE LAST FOREVER.

She tossed the magazine aside and rummaged through the pile. 'And look at all these. LOVE IN THE BIG CITY, SEASIDE ROMANCES CAN LAST. They're all about love and they're all lies and I hate them!'

Ruth could sense Gail getting over-excited again. 'You feel you've been let down?' she probed delicately.

'Look where love got me. I was going to go to college next year. I only let him do it to me 'cos he said he loved me. And we only did it once and now I'm having a baby. Is that love? Can't you get rid of it for me?'

'You've been through all this already, Gail. You know you agreed to carry on with the pregnancy. It's not much consolation now, but in time things will get better. You've got your whole life in front of you. You'll feel better later on.'

'You mean I might fall in love again? Never!'

There was a pause and Ruth wasn't quite sure what to say. Then Gail said in a quieter tone, 'My mother's been good but she doesn't like it. It worries her what the neighbours say.'

'It is difficult.' Ruth knew that there were two sides to living in a small community like Bannick. It could be very supportive, being surrounded by people who knew you. But the other side of it was that everybody knew everybody else's business. An idle thought flashed across her mind. She wondered if Micah knew how claustrophobic a small town could be.

'I'm sure your mother loves you.'

'Don't use that word!'

'I'm sorry. There are more kinds of love than one. Now, do you want me to run you home?'

But Gail was now feeling better. She'd arranged to meet a few schoolfriends for a coffee in town. Ruth extracted a promise that if she felt desperate again she'd phone the surgery. Then, wondering if a problem had been shelved rather than sorted out, she escorted the girl out of the building.

She felt slightly depressed as she walked back to the surgery. She could understand Gail's feeling that she had been trapped unfairly. For some reason the title of a fifties popular song and film she'd seen on TV clicked into her mind. 'Love is a Many-Splendored Thing'. Not for a lot of people it's not, she thought.

But her mood changed the minute she walked into Harry's room for coffee. Only Micah was there, and when he turned and smiled at her she felt suddenly, foolishly happy.

'Mary said you'd gone on an errand of mercy up the road,' he said. 'Here, have a coffee.'

With a sigh she collapsed next to him on the settee. 'Teenagers,' she said. 'Let's work out a system of having babies born aged twenty.'

He looked at her, obviously amused. 'What a thing to say. Now I don't know but I'm willing to bet that your teenage years were both hard-working and happy. Am I right?'

She sipped the coffee he handed her. 'I suppose so. What about yours?'

He shrugged. 'Hard-working certainly. I'm not too sure about happy.'

It was an odd, unsettling glimpse into his past and it reminded her how little she really knew about him. But before she could ask why he hadn't been happy he went on, 'But tell me about yesterday. How did you get on with the demon hockey player?'

'Evelyn? Pretty well. With any luck at all the tooth will be OK but she'll have a sore mouth for a day or two. I read the team the riot act about gum-shields.'

'Good. Most of the rugby team were wearing them.'

'I called back at the pitch and then I phoned to let you know,' she said. 'The Bell said that you'd been called urgently to Manchester.'

'Money problems,' he said. 'Not mine, but an old friend's. He needed some advice so I had to give it to him.'

'Did you manage to sort out his problems?'

He pursed his lips. 'I think so,' he said. 'It was just a matter of looking clearly at the situation and taking a decision, even though it was an unpleasant one.'

'But I thought you'd given up money dealing years ago.'

'I thought I had too,' he said ruefully. 'But our early deeds come back to haunt us. This man said he knew I was the only person who could help him. You can't escape your past, Ruth.'

'No,' she said thoughtfully, 'you can't escape your past.'

She looked at him levelly and he returned her gaze, unperturbed. 'In your past. . .' she started, but at that moment Harry and Martin walked in and she knew the moment was gone.

'Gossip—or news,' Harry announced as he made for the coffee-percolator. 'I think we'll have to organise some kind of a celebratory dinner. In six months' time Dr Samuel Parry will retire.'

'I don't believe it,' Ruth said. 'He's not sixty-five.'

'I thought he was eighty-five,' Martin put in, 'and no one'd noticed.'

Micah asked, 'I'm sorry, but who is this Dr Parry?'

'He's a doctor of the old school,' Harry said.

'He's a medical disgrace,' Martin said. 'He still thinks penicillin is a dangerous newfangled drug.'

'There's more to medicine than pills and potions, Martin,' Harry said cheerfully.

Seeing one of their amiable squabbles blowing up, and Micah still not understanding, Ruth moved to the map on the wall and pointed to the centre of town. 'Dr Parry's surgery is here,' she said. 'He works alone, out of his front room. He can walk to practically all his patients and he's known them all for years.'

'I admit he's been getting a bit tired recently,' Harry said, 'but he knows when people are ill and he refers them, and he knows that a few concerned words are often better than medicine.'

'I've never thought of him retiring,' Ruth said musingly. 'He's just part of the make-up of this town.'

'Who's going to take over his practice?' Micah asked suddenly. 'Why don't you apply to the Family Health Service Authority for his list?'

There was silence for a moment then he went on, 'It'd be a good opportunity to plan for the next twenty years or so. Sorry, I'm speaking out of turn. Not my job as trainee; I shouldn't interfere.'

Martin snorted. 'It's a really good idea. Dad, you've been saying for months now that we should do some forward planning and this would be the perfect opportunity.'

'Hmm,' Harry said. 'What do you think, Ruth?'

She didn't like it at all. Two minutes ago they'd been happily enjoying their coffee; now they were uprooting everything they'd built in the past years. She said, 'I think we're doing all right as we are. I'm happy with the present set-up and our patients seem happy enough too. Why change something that's working so well?'

'Because it won't carry on working well,' Martin said. 'We're not even coping with the paperwork at the moment.'

Ruth glanced angrily at Micah, the man who had started all this. He didn't even look her way and she felt a bit disregarded. However, she was determined not to get excited.

Putting her cup down with a snap, she said, 'I'm going to phone the social worker. I want a word about Gail Thompson.'

Micah turned to look at her impassively. His face never ceased to fascinate her. In a way it was ugly—certainly it wasn't conventionally handsome. It was usually vital, his eyes electric, his lips sensuous. But not always. He had this facility of shutting down, of assuming a bland, professional look that gave no indication of his feelings whatsoever. He had the mask on now. I bet that's how he used to look when he made lots of money, she thought fancifully. I'll bet he was ruthless.

Ruthless. She only realised that double meaning after the word floated to the surface of her mind. Why had she picked that word?

An hour later there was a tap on her door and Micah entered. 'Harry says you're going to see the parents of this girl, Gail Thompson. Would you mind if I came along? It's something I've never dealt with before and I'd like to see how it's done.'

'Love and its consequences,' Ruth said sourly. 'Yes, you can come with me. But let me do most of the talking.'

'Shall we take my car?' he asked.

Ruth had never treated either of Gail Thompson's parents before. But she got a pretty good idea of their character before she even entered the house.

For some reason Gail's story had affected her more than it should have. Ruth had learned early on the great danger of trying to live her patients' lives for them. A good GP was sympathetic, but ultimately detached. However, she could at least visit Gail's home.

The Thompsons lived in a neat terraced house. All the neighbours' houses looked well kept but the Thompsons' seemed to shine, from polished doorknob to heavy white-starched net curtains.

Ruth knocked. The door was opened by a woman, thin in face and body, wearing a spotless overall. 'Mrs Thompson? I'm Dr Francis and this is Dr North. I wonder if we might have a few words about Gail?'

'Does it take two of you? You'd better come in,' said Mrs Thompson, without smiling.

The front room was all Ruth had guessed it might be. Most of the furniture was thirty years old and shabby, but shone with polish and brushing. There was a television there so perhaps the family did use the room, but if they did they tidied it before they left. In the air was a heavy smell of room-freshener. Micah stood to one side and tried to look unobtrusive.

'Gail's lying down; I'll get her for you,' Mrs

Thompson said, still in the same monotone.

'Actually I wanted to talk to you.' Ruth moved over to close the door behind them. 'You look tired. This must have been a strain on you all.'

'Mr Thompson has a heart condition and he's not to be bothered. Your Dr Crowder told me that six months ago.'

'Where's Mr Thompson now?'

'In hospital for his check-up.'

'Perhaps as well under the circumstances. Now tell me how *you* are.'

For a moment Ruth thought the woman wasn't going to reply. Mrs Thompson's eyes flicked round the room, as if taking comfort from the gleaming brass ornaments, the sparkling mirror. Then, as if speaking to herself rather than to Ruth, she said, 'How could she do this to us? The shame would have killed my mother. We've always kept an eye on her, tried to bring her up right. I suppose we're old-fashioned. And now what will people say?'

'Does it matter what people say?'

For the first time Mrs Thompson's voice rose a little. 'You can ask that. You're not the one in trouble.' Then, more calmly, she went on, 'I've always tried to keep us respectable.'

'Have you made plans for the child?' Ruth asked cautiously.

'We'll do what's right by my daughter. But the baby will have to be adopted. It's a small house and I've two boys as well as Gail. We just couldn't cope. And although Gail's my own daughter I know she just doesn't have the sense to bring up a child.' For the first time the woman's shoulders shook. 'It's only five years since I bought her a blazer for her new school.'

'I gather you know the boy responsible?'

'His father has been to see me. I shut the door in his face. I want no charity!'

'It's hardly charity,' Ruth suggested. 'Perhaps he wants his son to do the right thing.'

'Well, he can't! He's only a child himself. I'll cope with my daughter. I want nothing from them.'

Ruth rose. 'Come and see me in the surgery in a day or so, Mrs Thompson. You're under strain and we'd like to make sure you're OK.' There was no answer so she went on, telling at least half a truth, 'I think Gail's very lucky to have such a supportive mother.'

There was no appreciation of the compliment. 'I do what I have to do.'

Ruth felt warmer as she stepped into the street.

'What are you going to do about Mrs Thompson?' Micah asked as they drove back to the surgery.

'Perhaps treat her for stress. See that her daughter and her child have medical care. Other than that there's nothing we can do.'

'Can't you advise her?'

'About how to live her life? It's dangerous. You can tell patients not to smoke. But you can't tell them not to marry a man you suspect is a dangerous psychopath.'

He thought for a moment. 'But in a small town like this you're going to have to live with your mistakes— say in the case of the psychopath.'

'I wouldn't have made a mistake! Because I wouldn't have done anything. For a doctor that's often the best course.'

'Harry says that,' he mused. 'He says that often the

best thing in medicine is to do nothing. The hard thing is deciding when.'

'Harry's a very good GP,' she said. She felt pleased that Micah was thinking about his work and realising that there was more to it than medicine.

'D'you mind if I go on my own to talk to Mrs Thompson?'

'You can certainly try. But, judging by your reception this time, I think she's off all men at the moment.'

'You may well be right,' he said thoughtfully.

'So I've outlined the main ideas put forward on the course. A lot of them I think are very good, and I've listed the ones we can put into action at once. Some of the others. . .well, I suggest we wait for a while.'

Ruth sat back with a sigh. She'd just finished the first of three meetings in which she intended to go over what she'd learned at the course on neonatal care. Now her two partners had to think about the suggestions and then the three of them would decide what to do. It was something they had to do carefully. There was no point in rushing.

Surprisingly it was Micah who came up with the first question. After leafing through his copy of the notes she'd provided he said, 'You suggest only implementing about half of the suggestions made on the course. What's wrong with the other ideas?'

She pursed her lips. 'We're a small country practice. I don't think we should rush into every newfangled system until we've seen how it works out.'

'You can be too cautious,' Harry said mildly. 'Anyway, I suggest we all read through this and have another meeting in a week or so. No point in talking about what we don't fully understand.'

Ruth thought it was a good idea. She knew Harry
had invited Micah to sit in on the meeting as a matter
of courtesy. But she wasn't sure he was entitled to
comment. Or was it that she didn't agree with what
he said?

For the rest of the week she hardly saw Micah at all.
It sometimes happened that way. He was spending
quite a bit of time with Harry; Ruth knew that Harry
took his duties as a trainer very seriously.

In a way this suited her. She could get her feelings
more under control. But she had to admit that when
they *did* bump into each other in the corridor, or their
fingers touched as he passed her a coffee, it gave her
a ridiculous amount of pleasure.

Once or twice they started a short, snatched semi-
intimate conversation but either the telephone or the
entrance of one of the partners stopped them
each time.

Then, on Friday morning, Ruth rang her bell for
what should have been the last of her patients—and
Micah walked in and sat in her patient's chair.

'Where's Mrs Bedford?' Ruth asked, looking at
her list.

'I finished early and I didn't think you'd mind if I
saw Mrs Bedford. We had a nice chat and I prescribed
some of those pink pills that do her so much good.'

'Well, thank you, you're a real doctor,' Ruth
acknowledged. She knew that was exactly what she'd
have done with the lady in question.

'Now, Doctor, I want a consultation.'

'What is it, Micah?' she asked uneasily.

'We have things to settle. We've started something and we have to talk about it. Besides—' his face lit with the smile that made her heart race '—I'm missing you.' After a pause he asked, 'Aren't you missing me?'

She pushed things around her desk, unwilling to meet his eyes. 'Perhaps I am a bit,' she said grudgingly. 'But I mustn't be rushed. I need time; you're confusing me.'

He shook his head. 'I don't think so. I think you're pushing me to the back of your mind, half hoping I'll go away. Well, I won't.'

The accuracy of this observation surprised her. She didn't even convince herself when she said, 'You're imagining things.'

'Possibly. You're on call on Sunday, aren't you?'

The roster was in front of her but she knew already. 'I am.'

'And I'm away to the big city tomorrow. But we're both free next Wednesday afternoon.'

Weakly she began, 'I was thinking of going to—'

'No, you weren't,' he interrupted. 'I'll be at your house at about two in the afternoon. We'll have all afternoon and all evening if necessary to sort things out. Will that be all right?'

After a pause she said, 'Perfectly.' She had a sense of being swept up towards some kind of climax. Whether she'd like it or not she didn't know.

# CHAPTER SIX

So Micah was coming to see her.

He wasn't at the surgery all Wednesday morning. When she asked, Martin mumbled something about him doing something for Harry. She didn't have too many patients, perhaps because it was another glorious beginning-of-summer day with the warm sunshine cooled by the gentlest of breezes. She left early, and once back home, to keep herself busy, she pottered about, plumping cushions and putting her many books and records in order. She didn't need to—her home was always tidy—but it gave her something to do.

She wondered if she should expect him to stay. If so, she had the makings of a light meal. He had said that he'd be here by two o'clock and they'd have all afternoon and evening to sort things out. She felt both apprehensive and excited at the thought. What did he mean?

It had been hard but so far she had managed to put off thinking about him. By 'thinking' she meant sitting down, considering their relationship logically and coldly and not moving until she'd reached a firm decision. It didn't mean remembering the curve of his cheek or the colour of his eyes when she first woke up in the morning. It didn't mean imagining what it would be like if he kissed her again as he had the evening of the ball. In spite of herself, she'd done quite a lot of that.

But for all her determination her heart still thumped when her doorbell rang. And when she opened the door she blinked. Glowing green eyes and the smile showed how pleased he was to see her. But he was dressed. . .

'You're wearing shorts,' she said.

'The sun's out, the weather's warm—why don't you join me?' After a pause he said, 'May I come in?'

'I'm sorry! I was just surprised at. . . Please do come in.'

She had seen him in a suit or sports jacket at the surgery, in the black and white splendour of evening dress, even in anorak and boots while walking. But this casual dress was something else. He wore a white T-shirt, smart blue shorts and walking boots. She could see muscular calves and thighs covered by the finest of dark down, and tanned, well-shaped arms.

He entered and sat in the chair she indicated. The sheer physicality of him was a sudden shock. He'd been here before, of course, but now he was—she gulped at the thought—half-naked.

He sat in her wooden rocking chair, relaxed and at home. There was a tiny regular squeak as he rocked backwards and forwards. She didn't know what to say.

'I've brought a bit of a picnic from the Bell,' he said. 'We should take advantage of the good weather so I thought we might go for a walk. Nothing too ambitious. D'you fancy it?'

For some reason she hadn't thought of this. But the more she thought about it, the better the idea seemed. She loved walking and there was no one she'd rather walk with than Micah. And if they had to talk, exercise would make any decisions more acceptable.

'That's a brilliant idea,' she said. 'I'll go and get changed. Do you want a drink before we go?'

'Not unless you do. I'd like to get off at once. We've been working too hard; we need to get on top of something.'

As she headed for the bedroom he called, 'We're not going anywhere too high. If you wear shorts too, then I won't feel such a fool.'

'You don't feel a fool,' she muttered to herself, but she put on a pair of shorts anyway.

'Where are we going?' she asked as they drove out of the village.

'Let me surprise you. I've been studying the map, trying to find a route that's beautiful but well away from civilisation. I'm beginning to realise that every doctor needs just a little time away from people.'

'I think you're right,' she agreed, 'but it takes most newcomers to the profession a while to realise it.'

He laughed. 'Not me. In finance I saw a lot of people burn out without realising it. They started to make mistakes—and that was the end.'

She felt a momentary touch of doubt. Every now and then he said something that showed her there was so much about him that she didn't know. Not only that, but so much she felt she could never understand. He was almost a creature from another world.

For the moment she was content to be driven. Sitting in the Range Rover, she was much higher than in her Escort, and she was surprised at how much more she could see. But she knew that this period of peace could not last.

Quietly he asked, 'Do we walk then talk, or talk then walk, or amalgamate the two? I don't want to push you, Ruth, but I think there are things we have to say.'

'I suppose so. In fact I know so.'

From somewhere she gathered the self-possession that seemed to have been lacking over the past few days. This was going to be one of the most difficult conversations she'd ever had. But she had to get things clear.

He seemed to sympathise with her plight, to understand instinctively what she was going through. He said, 'It's hard, isn't it, Ruth, trying to be open when you've spent your life being wary? Believe me, I know it; I've been through it myself.'

With mock solemnity he lifted his hand from the steering wheel and said, 'To encourage you I was going to rest my hand on your leg—in a purely friendly gesture, of course. But your leg is naked! A man's intentions could be misunderstood. So if I give you a sociable little pat all will be well.'

He gave her a sociable little pat. She wondered if he knew what a torrent of emotions was caused by the touch of his warm hand. But his humour helped her to start.

'That Saturday, at the summer ball, I had two of the biggest shocks of my life. I found out I was vulnerable—vulnerable to you. You affected me in a way I hadn't been for years; you made me feel like a full woman again and I glimpsed what I'd been missing for so long. It was wonderful. And I thought I was made of iron.

'Then I found out that—in some sense—you'd been deceiving me. I know it's silly, I should be pleased that you're so rich, but I felt cheated. Almost as if you were married or something. Something very important between us you hadn't even mentioned. Suddenly you were a stranger, not the man I thought I might fall for. Now I don't know what to feel.'

There was silence for a while. She turned to look at him directly; for once he wasn't hiding his thoughts behind the bland mask she'd seen so often. He looked troubled.

After some time he reached out and touched her thigh again, a light, stroking gesture that she recognised instinctively as being intended to comfort. 'I made a decision to keep quiet,' he said. 'Perhaps it was the wrong one, but I made it in good faith.'

'I'm sure you did,' she said quietly.

'How have you managed the last few days? You've seemed fine at work—though sometimes I've seen you looking at me and I've wondered what you were thinking.'

Once again she marvelled at his shrewdness, his powers of observation. Did nothing escape him? She'd thought her secret glances had been well hidden.

'I'm Dr Ruth Francis. I cope. It's a technique I developed after Matt's death. If I'd let myself I would never have stopped thinking about him. But I had a job to do. I didn't take the time off offered by Harry; I went straight to work and ignored the whisperings and the well-meant sympathy. Not a single one of my patients suffered because of Matt's death.'

She took a deep breath. What she had described was true, but thinking of it again reminded her of what it had cost her.

'You cut yourself off from all emotional reaction. Are you sure it was a good idea?'

'I'm not so sure now, but it's the way I've always been. I wept into my pillow every night for six months, but no one knew. You're the only person I've ever told.' After a pause she said, 'And it's made it easier to deal with you.'

'I see,' he sighed, and she smiled.

'Don't worry. All I'm saying is I need time. I'm still suspicious of sudden decisions and changes in my life.'

'Life is decision and change,' he offered. 'Surely medicine teaches you that?'

She grinned. 'Harry says the only thing forty years of practising medicine has taught him is that he knows less now than when he started.'

He responded to her forceful change of mood. 'What shall I do about you, Ruth?' he asked. 'Things were better a hundred years ago. I could have come courting as you sat knitting in your parlour with a big-moustached dad looking at me.' He adopted a broad Yorkshire accent. '"Na' then, lad, what dost want wi' mi daughter? And has tha' got any brass?"'

He turned and winked at her. 'And I should say, I am in possession of a small competence, sir. And I assure you my intentions are purely honourable.'

They laughed together. Both realised there was much more to be said, but for the moment it was good to relax.

They'd been travelling for nearly an hour, penetrating the heart of the Lake District. Micah had worked out a route that took them off the main roads and for some time now they'd been following a lane barely wide enough for their vehicle.

The lane ran alongside a wood, dark with Forestry Commission conifers. Micah stopped, peered at his map, then drove another hundred yards to bump onto a path that led deep into the forest. After five minutes of spine-jarring driving they reached a little clearing, and he stopped. 'The walk begins,' he said.

Ruth climbed out, feeling rather excited. 'I've no idea where we are,' she said, 'but it's going to be fun finding out.'

He obviously shared her enthusiasm. 'I'm looking forward to it too.' He slung a rucksack on his back and took a book and a pair of binoculars from under his seat. 'Trafalgar Square is full of pigeons, but the countryside is full of all sorts of birds. I can recognise a sparrow, a crow and a robin. With my binoculars and my little book I intend to do better. You can help me. What's that?'

Across from them a small dark bird flew from one rock to another, showing a white underside. Micah studied it for a moment then handed the binoculars to Ruth as he flicked through his little book.

'That, I think, is a wheatear.' He took out a pencil and scribbled in the margin. 'Officially noted today. This is going to be more fun than spotting railway trains.'

Ruth laughed. It was hard to remember that this man, with such obvious schoolboy enthusiasm, was both a doctor and a millionaire. 'You're an idiot,' she said affectionately. 'Now, take me up this hill.'

There was some sort of path which wound steeply up through the trees. They followed it carefully. After fifteen minutes both were glad to stop; the incline was steeper than it seemed. They collapsed onto a felled log.

After two minutes Ruth felt her heartbeat slow to

an acceptable level. She remembered that there was something she had to say. 'Micah, coming here we just talked about me. You were left out. I bared my soul and I need to know that you'll do the same.'

'If I can get my breath back first,' he gasped. But when he looked at her a moment later his eyes were sincere. 'That's fair enough. There are things I want to say to you but I don't want to go into them now. Shall we wait?'

'We'll wait.' She smiled and stood. 'Now move before you stiffen up.'

'You're a slave-driver.'

They set off again.

The path eased off shortly afterwards and then there was a stile at the edge of the wood and the prospect of open country beyond. Micah climbed over the stile first and held Ruth's hand as she jumped. Once she was over he didn't let go and she looked down at their joined hands.

'Do you remember Murphy's law from college?' she asked.

He shook his head, puzzled. 'Afraid not.'

'It's the truest of all natural laws. It states that whatever can go wrong will go wrong. If you hold my hand half a dozen of our patients will suddenly appear round the corner.'

'So what? Does it matter?'

'It certainly does. We're country doctors. We're pillars of the community, not members of the human race. We don't have money troubles, drink problems, sex lives. Our cars always start and we're not allowed to be ill.'

He looked at her in mock horror. 'I wonder if I've

chosen the right job. I want to be a doctor, not half saint, half superman.'

Gently she took her hand from his. Then she reached up and kissed him on the cheek. She wasn't sure why; she just had a sudden flash of pure happiness and wanted to share it.

'You kissed me,' he said.

'I wanted to so I did. Just a sudden impulse.'

'I didn't think you acted on impulse.'

'It's very rarely that I do. But the sun's shining, birds are singing and the walk ahead looks much easier. I felt happy so I kissed you.'

He looked at her gravely. Then, as he turned to stride on, he reached out his hand to her. She took it.

They walked away from the woodland onto a broad, bare ridge. Thin, sheep-cropped grass was springy underneath their feet and on each side of them there were magnificent views down into the valleys below. Micah had chosen well; there wasn't another person in sight. Ruth sighed with happiness.

The ridge stretched away into the distance, where they could just see a cairn. It grew warmer as they walked and she stopped to take off her thin anorak and tie it round her waist. Micah took off his shirt, then seized his binoculars as a dark bird flew low over the grass ahead of them.

She took the chance to stare at his body, unobserved. For a moment she pretended to herself that she was examining him dispassionately, as a doctor. It didn't work. Honesty took over and she inwardly acknowledged the thrill he gave her.

His skin was smooth, but across his chest were two great wings of fine brown hair that thinned and disappeared into the top of his shorts. The muscles of his shoulders, chest and abdomen were well etched; he showed no sign of fat. She wondered if. . .

Suddenly he dropped his binoculars and saw her staring. 'There's a lot to look at up here,' he said mischievously. 'I've seen two birds I can't name.'

She blushed slightly. 'You keep fit,' she said. 'I can tell.'

'I always have done. I'd rather go without food than exercise. Keeping fit makes me feel good, and I like that.'

'I know what you mean.'

When they walked on he took her hand again. But now she was ever conscious of his half-nakedness beside her. From time to time his shoulder brushed her bare arm and she could just detect the exciting musky scent of his skin.

They spoke little. Both seemed content with their silent togetherness. They were two people alone, tiny figures on a green carpet under the great blue arch of the sky. She couldn't recollect ever being so pleased to be alive.

'We've been walking for quite a while,' Micah said eventually, breaking into their companionable silence. 'Are you hungry yet?'

She *was* hungry. She'd been so happy with the walk that she'd forgotten about food, but now that he'd spoken she realised that she hadn't eaten since breakfast. 'Yes, I am,' she admitted.

'It's time we had a rest anyway. We'll see what the Bell has put up for us.'

He led her off the ill-defined path on the ridge, down to a tiny outcrop of rocks. There was an alcove, sheltering them from view on three sides and with only the long slope down to a lake in the valley in front of them.

To one side was the beginning of a tiny stream. Ruth took off her boots and socks to dabble her feet and shuddered when they touched the icy water. 'Now that is a good idea,' he said, and with a grin did the same.

From his rucksack he took a silver groundsheet and a blanket and spread them both in the alcove. Then he opened assorted plastic boxes. 'Come and sit down,' he said. 'I told the Bell exactly what I wanted so if you don't like anything you can blame me.'

Two pairs of boots stood by the stream. She came to sit and peer. 'It all looks magnificent,' she said.

There were crusty buttered rolls and the thinnest of dark rye bread. Smoked salmon, chicken breast and cheese were in another container, with a green salad and a little phial of dressing. In one Thermos was freshly pressed orange juice; in another was coffee.

They sat and ate silently. The meal was just right; he hadn't fallen into the trap of ordering too much. When she had finished she dabbed her mouth with a napkin as he cleared away. 'That was wonderful,' she said. 'I didn't know you were such an expert caterer.'

'There are lots of things about me you don't know,' he agreed. 'I'm hoping you'll find out in time.'

'Perhaps,' she said sleepily. 'You don't want to move on straight away, do you?'

'I want to do what you want.'

'Then we'll stay here for a while longer. Sometimes I think we rush about too much. It's a good idea to relax, to have a rest occasionally.'

'I don't believe this is the super-efficient, ever working Dr Francis talking.'

'There are a lot of things about me you don't know,' she retorted. 'Now for ten minutes I'm going to do exactly nothing.'

She lay back and closed her eyes. Under the blanket the grass made a perfect bed and pillow. The sun warmed her but wasn't too hot and she sighed with contentment. He stretched out by her side. For a moment she stiffened as his bare foot rubbed against her leg, but then she relaxed again. Just an accident, she decided.

Perhaps ten minutes later she woke, but didn't open her eyes. It hadn't been a real sleep but she felt refreshed.

There was the faintest of sensations on her face. It moved across her forehead and down her cheek to follow the curve of her upper lip. 'You're tickling me,' she said drowsily.

'Don't you like it?'

'Mmm. I think so.'

He bent forward again and drew the blade of grass further down her chin. She still wasn't fully awake. The grass had the gentlest of touches, soothing rather than exciting. He drew it slowly upwards, across the line of her jaw to touch her ear. She breathed more deeply; her ear was sensitive. Then he moved on to her forehead again and down between her eyes to touch her nose and outline her lips.

The grass didn't move again and she missed its delicate caress. She frowned. 'That's nice, don't stop,' she said, her dreamy voice indicating that she still didn't want to wake up.

'If you want me not to stop,' he said. There was something in the quality of his voice that struck her as perhaps being important, but she couldn't be bothered with it now.

The gentle touch started again. But this time it wasn't a blade of grass but a fingertip. She didn't mind; it was just as pleasant. With his finger he traced the same path as before, touching lips, cheeks, forehead and down again. His finger hesitated then traced the angle of her jaw, circling down under her chin to her shoulder, where it ran along the line of her shirt.

He stopped again. She felt him move and the glow of the sun, through her still closed eyes, was suddenly darkened. He leaned over her. She could feel his head coming closer to hers and there was the sweet warmth of his breath on her cheek. His head bowed and his lips touched hers, with the same soft touch as the grass.

'I like that,' she said reproachfully as he moved his head away, but he didn't move back to kiss her again. Instead he put his hand on her cheek and stroked it. Then he followed the line of her jaw again, down her neck until his fingers rested on the edge of her shirt.

It was an invitation and a question and it was up to her to respond. She had to make some kind of a commitment. Reaching up to feel for the buttons on the front of her shirt, she undid them one by one. Then her hands fell back by her sides.

Slowly his hand slipped under her shirt, outlining the curves there. Her shirt fell back and she shivered as his fingertip traced a line between her breasts. Then she smiled. Her bra fastened at the front. She didn't want to roll over or be tugged at; she wanted to remain in this delicious floating state in which nice things happened to her and she didn't have to do much to help.

There was the faintest of clicks as he deftly undid her bra. Then she felt him push the dainty white lace to the side. She sighed deeply.

For a moment he did nothing and she lay there, suspended in happy semiconsciousness. Then, to her mild surprise, he leaned over to kiss her lips again.

At first it was the most delicate of touches again. But then his kiss grew harder and more insistent. She felt his tongue on the soft skin on the inside of her lips and her mouth opened to receive him.

He took his mouth from hers and kissed her on each cheek. Then he kissed her chin, her throat, and his head descended on her breast.

Ruth was asleep no longer. She breathed heavily, feeling the blood racing through her body. He kissed her breasts in turn, his tongue seeking the pink tips. They grew hard, and she writhed and arched her back at the exquisite sensation.

'My Ruth,' she heard him say, and he twisted to lie on top of her, holding her head between his hands, his mouth devouring hers. Her arms wrapped round him, clutched him tightly. She pushed her half-naked body up against his, feeling the hardness of his muscles, the fine hair on his chest rubbing against her nipples and making them peak with desire.

For a while she wanted nothing but this. But then she realised that for her sake he was holding back. His body was pressed close to hers and even though they both wore shorts his maleness was obvious.

'Ruth, I want you, I want to. . .' he breathed, his voice hoarse with passion.

'I want you too,' she whispered back. 'You'll have. . .you'll have to help me.'

She felt his hesitancy and, with a daring she didn't know she possessed, took her arms from round his back and fumbled to undo the clip on her shorts.

He kissed her again—a long, lingering kiss—and then she felt his hands on her hips, sliding off shorts and briefs. She heard the rustle of his clothing and for a moment squeezed her eyes shut in fear. She had not meant to go this far!

Micah was slow, gentle, considerate. His hands, his lips roamed her body till she forgot her momentary fear and her body relaxed, wanting him, willing him to come to her.

She groaned as unimagined sensations flooded through her, making her wonder if she'd been spending her time up to now only half-alive. So sweet was her pleasure that it came almost as a shock to realise that they were not yet fully together, but then, with the tiniest of pains, she became fully a woman again.

She responded to his urgency, thrusting her body against his until she cried, 'Micah, oh, my Micah,' in a tide of passion that swept her into ecstasy. She heard his cry of delight and felt his body surge frantically against hers. Then there was stillness and silence. Breathless, he leaned his head on her breast and she held him there.

She closed her eyes and saw an image of a still, silent pool of water. A stone splashed into the centre and ripples spread from it—to end she knew not where.

After a while the tears came and he sat beside her, holding her, pulling the blanket around them both. 'I don't cry,' she sobbed. 'Or if I do it's because I'm happy.'

He said nothing, only pulling her closer to him, and after a while the fit passed. He reached for his shorts and passed her a handkerchief. She wiped her eyes.

'Just for a minute I'm going to be a doctor,' she said, giving him a tremulous smile. 'Are there likely to be any consequences of this behaviour?'

'Quite a lot, I hope,' he said. 'But if you mean medical consequences, then no. I took precautions.'

'I'm glad,' she said. 'I've got enough to think about.'

He now sat with his back against the rock and she nestled with her back to his chest and his arms around her, both wrapped in the blanket. She gazed contentedly at the scene around them, the long, lonely stretches of grass, the lake far below, the hazy distant horizon.

After a while he bowed his head and kissed her on the nape of her neck. She wondered that after all she'd just experienced the caress could give her such pleasure.

'You're about to say something disagreeable,' he said. 'Your body's gone all taut and I can feel you trying to work out the right words.'

Perceptive again! She pulled one of his arms to her and kissed the back of his hand. 'Not disagreeable,' she said, 'but practical or something. I think we ought to get dressed.'

'But I love the feel of you naked.'

Quietly she said, 'And I love the feel of you too. Let's stay like this for another five minutes.'

As answer he kissed her neck again.

'Did you plan this?' she asked after a while. 'I'm

not objecting, because I was obviously willing, but is it why you brought me here?'

She could feel him shake his head, his chest pressing closer to her back. 'No. I wanted to be alone with you and I've dreamed of something like this happening but I didn't plan it.' He chose his words carefully. 'I'll not ask did you mind—but are you sorry we did it now?'

She twisted round and pressed her lips to his, amused at his expression of surprise. 'No,' she said, 'I'm not sorry.'

Then, taking him by surprise, she rolled to her feet to stand proud and naked in front of him. She lifted her arms to reach to the sky.

'That was one of the most wonderful things that has ever happened to me,' she said.

She smiled as she watched him looking up at her body. Without false modesty she knew she looked well; like many tall women she looked better naked than dressed. 'We'd better get dressed,' she said.

## CHAPTER SEVEN

WHEN they were both dressed Micah packed the groundsheet and blanket back into his rucksack. Ruth watched him, enjoying the neatness of his movements. Then he slung the pack onto his back. 'We must come back here,' he said, surveying the tiny alcove, the bubbling stream, 'in memory of happy times.'

'Come on, you.' She thumped him affectionately on the back. Hand in hand they walked back to the ridge, where he checked his watch and looked at the map.

'I'd still like to finish the walk and get up to the cairn,' he said, pointing to the high point of the ridge. 'Having come so far it would be a pity not to get there.'

She didn't care either way, but wanted to make him happy. As they set off towards it she asked, 'Do you always have to finish what you start?'

It was a half-joking question but he took it seriously. 'I know it can be a fault. Sometimes I push things to a conclusion when they might have been better left alone. Obsessive behaviour is unreasonable. I can only say I'm better than I was.'

She wasn't sure what to make of this admission.

They reached the cairn, admired the view again and set off back. She revelled in the sun on her face and his strong hand holding hers. But she knew this feeling of elation couldn't last. She had started the walk wondering what to do about Micah. She'd talked about it frankly to him. But now the problem was—well, not worse, but different.

Sensing her change of mood, he said, 'You're quiet, Ruth. I hope you're not regretting what we did?'

She shook her head. 'No. I was a more than willing partner. Something tremendous happened to me but I'm not yet sure what it was.'

'Something tremendous happened to *us*,' he corrected her. 'Whatever it was, I want to be a part of it.'

'I know,' she said. 'I can see you think I'm being selfish, but it's the way I am.'

He squeezed her hand in reply, but said nothing.

To her surprise she found that she could be philosophical about the affair. Some part of her brain enabled her to detach herself from what she'd done and its possible consequences.

'I know men are different,' she said. 'We had a gynae consultant at the hospital where I trained called Mavis Dixon. She used to tell us that when it came to reproduction and the assorted trauma before, during and after, men and women were totally different creatures. For a start, how clever of God to ensure that men didn't have babies.'

He smiled. 'I've heard of the woman,' he said. 'She's been married four times.'

'Obviously not going to stop until she gets things right. That way madness lies.'

He shook his head. 'That's not madness, it's determination. There's a lot to be said for it. If you see what you want, then go for it.'

'I wonder,' she said thoughtfully.

For the rest of the walk they said little, content to appreciate the beauty of the afternoon in silence. Only

when they reached the Range Rover did he speak
seriously to her again. First he kissed her on the forehead. Then he said, 'Ruth, you must know that
whatever we shared meant as much to me as I think
it did to you. Whatever you're thinking, you must
remember that.'

Ruth knew he was telling the truth; he deserved an
honest answer. 'You're starting something in me I
don't know if I want. I've been madly in love before
and it only meant pain to me. I've been quietly content
for some time now; I don't know if I want the
excitement.'

Wisely, he said nothing.

She skimmed through his tape collection as they drove
away, then turned to ask him if there was anything he
particularly wanted to listen to. The answer was
prompt. 'Beethoven's Ninth Symphony. The triumph
of the human spirit over adversity. I love it.'

She grinned. 'Are you trying to say something to
me?'

'You bet I am. I especially like the last movement—
the "Hymn to Joy". Whenever I'm joyful I like to sing
a hymn.'

'I'll bet you do,' she said. For the rest of the journey
they let the music swell around them.

It was still quite early when he drew up in front of
her cottage. At the front door she turned to him.
'Don't take this the wrong way, Micah, but I'm not
inviting you in. I've got a lot of thinking to do. If you
stay with me now I'm likely to say something or do
something that we both might regret.'

'I suppose that's fair. But remember, Ruth, you can't

just think of yourself. You've got to think of me too.'
Then he was gone.

She went upstairs, bathed and changed into an old
tracksuit. Then, with a great cheese sandwich and a
mug of cocoa, she lay on her couch and forgot about
Micah North. It was something she'd seen before in
patients, a kind of emotional overload in which an
over-stressed mind rejected any further commitment.
After laughing for an hour at a television comedy film,
she went to bed and slept soundly till morning.

Next morning she took refuge in the fact that she was
a doctor. It was a kind of escape, but she needed it.
She dressed in a severe blue suit, made sure her
chignon was tight, her make-up subdued but perfect.
Holding her briefcase like a badge of office, she walked
into the surgery.

She was very early, the first doctor to arrive. As she
passed the receptionist's desk, calling hello, Mary said,
'We've got an urgent case. Wanted to come here
instead of going to hospital. I've given him a cup of tea
and told him not to bleed on the waiting-room floor.'

'Bleed?' asked Ruth. 'Give me a minute to put on
a white coat and send him in.'

In a way she was relieved. Having an emergency
before surgery could be a nuisance but it would give
her something to do, reinforce her view of herself as
a doctor before she had to meet Micah again.

There was a tap on the door and Mary ushered in
the emergency, a burly middle-aged man dressed in a
brown warehouse coat. There were bloodstains on his
coat and on the white dressing wrapped roughly round
his hand. Ruth recognised him; he was an assistant

manager at the grocer's in the high street. Her eyes flicked to the name on the card laid on her desk by Mary.

'Sit down here, Mr Vincent,' she said calmly. 'Sorry you've had to wait. You should have gone to the hospital casualty department.'

He tried a weak smile. 'Too far away and you have to wait even longer there. If you can fix this I can get back to work.'

She rested the injured hand on a table and slipped on rubber gloves before carefully unwrapping the blood-encrusted bandages. She noted the unsteadiness in his voice and his pale face.

'You'll be going straight home when I've dressed this,' she said. 'Someone will have to take you.'

'But it's stocktaking and I'm needed!'

'You'll be no use to anyone if you keep on fainting. How did you do this?'

She'd finally laid bare the injury, a long cut stretching from his wrist down the back of his hand. It looked nasty but it wasn't too deep and she felt that she could suture it without too much trouble.

'A packing case fell. It had a bit of metal sticking out of the side.'

She stooped to examine the wound. There was no evidence of bruising. 'It didn't actually fall on your hand? Your hand wasn't squashed?'

'No. In fact I didn't notice it was bleeding for a while.'

She nodded. 'That quite often happens with a clean cut. You've got no other injuries? No other pains?'

'Well, I don't feel too good but I guess I'm all right.'

'Good. This will take a while but there's no great

damage to your hand.' First she injected lignocaine at each side of the gash. Then there was a ten-minute wait for the local anaesthetic to take effect. She laid out all she would need—scissors, forceps, a needle holder and 5.0. silk sutures. Then there was a kidney bowl with cotton wool and Savlodil for cleaning.

After that it was painstaking, delicate, but ultimately satisfying work, cleaning the exposed tissue, pulling the skin back in place and suturing it. A final dressing strapped into place and he was done.

'You should go straight home and rest, Mr Vincent. Can you phone for someone to take you?'

'Someone from work will come. Er, thanks, Doctor. I'm glad I didn't have to go to hospital.'

She smiled. 'Make an appointment to come and see the nurse in five days and she'll have a look at those stitches. Bye, Mr Vincent.'

When he'd gone she glanced at her watch. Two minutes late starting surgery. She thought of the job she'd just finished. Nothing too exciting or difficult, but a good job well done. She felt pleased with herself. It was good to be a doctor. She rang for the first patient.

Today she had a fuller list than normal. Halfway through the morning Mary slipped in with a cup of coffee and an explanation. 'Dr Harry came and said he'd sent Dr North to Leeds on an errand. You're all taking his patients.'

'That's funny,' said Ruth, wondering why Harry would do such a thing.

Mary went on, 'And there's a Mr Smart phoned asking if he could have an appointment with you. He's not on our list and he said he wouldn't mind coming privately. I'm to phone him back.'

'Privately?' asked Ruth. She had no private patients. 'What does he want, Mary?'

'He wouldn't say. Isn't someone called Smart the father of young Gail Thompson's baby?'

'That's right.' Once again Ruth realised that Mary was better informed than any computer. 'Is it the father, d'you think?'

Mary shook her head. 'Far too old.'

'Ask him to come and see me after surgery, Mary, will you?' Ruth decided not to speculate about the purpose of the visit.

Five minutes after the last patient had been dealt with, Mary rang to announce that a Mr Smart was here. Ruth could now read the undercurrents of Mary's voice. Whatever had happened to Gail Thompson, Mary approved of Mr Smart.

Ruth saw why at once. Mr Smart was about fifty, probably rich, well dressed, and sincere. With an inward smile she noted his look of approval as he saw her blue suit and freshly arranged chignon. Mr Smart obviously liked things to be proper. He shook her hand and accepted the offered chair.

'I'm James Smart, Doctor. I'm the father of Jerry Smart who is in turn the father of the baby Gail Thompson is expecting.'

'I see. Let me make it clear that there is no way I can talk about one of my patients without her consent.'

'I understand. Will you talk to me about my son, Jerry?'

Ruth thought for a moment, then, 'I'm not very happy about it,' she said, 'but we can try.'

He grimaced. 'I didn't realise how difficult talking

could be. I tried to talk to Gail's mother but she shut the door in my face. I couldn't get much sense out of the social worker either. It might be my fault but I can't talk to a woman who looks as if she's come from an African kraal, not main-street Bannick.'

Ruth actually felt that Alice—'call me Al'—Seymour's outfit of batik print and wooden beads looked quite attractive. She got across to her younger clients. But she could see what Mr Smart meant.

'I want to tell you, Doctor, that Jerry, my son, will face up to all his responsibilities. Not only money—I've got plenty of that—but anything else he can do. My wife and I like Gail; we'd like to help her. But her mother won't hear of it.'

'Is there any possibility of their getting married?'

He shook his head. 'I've thought of it but it would be a short cut to disaster. He's my son and I love him, but I know he's hopelessly immature. The situation would only get worse.'

'I see.' She decided to keep quiet a moment, to see what he would say next.

After a while he went on, 'Jerry's our only child; my wife couldn't have any more though she dearly wanted to. This will be our first grandchild. I'd like to do something for it before he or she slips out of our lives.'

Carefully Ruth said, 'Gail is one of our patients. I can tell you that we're aware of the situation and that she'll get all the help, medical and otherwise, that we can give her.'

'I've no doubt about that, Doctor! No doubt at all.'

She found herself feeling sorry for this man, obviously decent and not knowing what to do. But her powers as a doctor were limited. 'I don't think I can usefully say any more,' she said. 'I can pass on your offer of financial assistance but whether it's accepted or not is not up to me.'

There was silence for a moment. 'What will happen to the baby?' he asked.

Ruth knew that the baby would almost certainly be adopted but the information wasn't hers to give. 'That will be up to Gail and her family to decide.'

He knew what that meant. 'I see,' he said sadly. He rose to go. 'If there's anything I can do, or any way you can help me, you'll let me know?'

'It'll be a pleasure, Mr Smart. But I can't offer much hope.'

He shook hands and left.

Only Martin was drinking coffee when she went to Harry's room. He poured her a cup and passed the biscuits. 'Why so gloomy, Ruth?'

She slumped into a chair. 'I feel old. You know Gail Thompson—the seventeen-year-old pregnancy case? Well, I've just had her boyfriend's father in. And I feel sorrier for him than I do for the kids involved.'

Martin smiled. 'We're doctors, Ruth. We don't get too involved.'

'I suppose not. Well, I'm late for my calls.'

Only as she left did she realise that she'd forgotten to ask where Micah was. His absence was both a relief and a disappointment. She felt she ought to have a period of calmness, a rest from the searing passions she'd experienced yesterday. But she also knew that she longed to see him.

Her calls didn't take long, and as she walked down the busy high street—saying hello, it seemed, to every third person—she met young George Miller. He greeted her cheerfully, took her arm and pulled her to one side. He wanted a chat.

'How's your father, George?' she asked. She had every doctor's dislike of providing roadside diagnoses, but she'd known the family for years.

'He's great, Ruth, just great. Ma says he's a lot easier to live with now he's taking those pills. Just wanted to let you know.'

'He's not doing too much?'

Young George shook his head. 'Reckon he's learned his lesson. Just comes down the yard to mither me, but that's all. Ma says call again when you've time and let her know first. Aye, and bring that other doctor. Ma says she'll have a chicken for each of you.'

'I'll be round soon, don't worry.' She made her way back to her car feeling a little happier.

She'd only just got the key in her front door when Albert called her. This was strange; usually he preferred to wait so that he could come inside. It must be something important.

'Ruthie! There's some flowers for you! Came this afternoon when you were out.'

Albert dived back inside his own cottage door and reappeared with a vast bunch of roses. Ruth sighed. They could only be from Micah. Didn't he know anything about living in the country? Now everyone in her village would know she'd received flowers. And everyone knew—or thought they knew—what that meant.

As Albert approached, she winced. This was no ordinary bunch ordered from the high street. There were red, white and yellow flowers, each individual bud perfect. Albert, who grew his own flowers, knew this as well and surveyed Ruth mistrustfully. 'These aren't English,' he said darkly. 'Had to come from abroad. That cost an awful lot of money.'

She opened her door and he followed her, carrying the bouquet. He laid it carefully on her table and stood expectantly as she reached for the little envelope attached to it. It opened surprisingly easily. Fortunately the message inside was sufficiently inconclusive. 'With thanks for a wonderful walk and everything— Micah.' Perhaps he was a little more aware than she realised.

'It's from our new trainee,' she explained to Albert. 'We went walking yesterday.'

'Trainee?' Albert indicated that he'd never heard it called that before.

'You know, the man who picked me up in the dinner suit last week.'

'Oh, him!' Albert's eyes lit up and he left, to present his wife with this latest titbit.

Ruth separated the roses into three bunches and set them in vases round her room. They looked splendid and she loved them. She understood Albert's surprise. Sending flowers like this wasn't typical behaviour in Bannick. It was the act of a rich, urbane sophisticate. What would she do with such a man?

Next morning she found out. Micah stepped out of his room just as she arrived. There was a sudden rush of feelings and memories and as she looked at him, smart and professionally dressed, she remembered how they'd been on the mountaintop. Her cheekbones felt slightly warm.

'Ruth, good morning! Have you got a minute?

I've had a letter I'd like you to look at.'

She stopped, confused. 'Just nip into my room,' he invited, and she did.

The minute the door was closed behind them she found herself wrapped in his arms and very soundly kissed.

At first she struggled but he was too strong for her so she gave way. She enjoyed it—but there was a time and place for everything. 'Micah! We're at work!' she muttered furiously when he finally released her.

It didn't seem to bother him. 'Surgery starts in exactly a minute and a half,' he said. 'Ninety seconds put to good use is ninety seconds saved.'

'You sound like my old headmistress,' she grumbled. 'What is this letter, anyway?'

He winked. 'Actually it's a bill from my tailor. Any excuse to get you alone is a good one.'

'You're incorrigible,' she said, and made for the door. Turning there, she said, 'And trainee doctors shouldn't have lipstick on their cheek.' It wasn't much of a last word, but it would have to do.

'There's another thing,' he called. 'Harry wants a full practice meeting for an hour after surgery this evening. It's important that you come.'

'An hour? What's going to take so long?' Because they all saw each other so regularly it was seldom necessary to meet formally.

His face took on that bland expression that could mean so much or so little. Faint unease stirred through her. 'We'll know at the meeting,' he said. 'See you there.' She'd been dismissed. Thoughtfully she went to her own room.

\*     \*     \*

It was a busy day and she hardly saw anyone before the evening. But she managed to get to Harry's room a little early and found him alone there. He seemed preoccupied. Just as she was about to ask why he'd called them together he spoke first. 'What d'you think of Micah, Ruth? Will he make a good doctor?'

She looked at him suspiciously but there didn't seem to be any ulterior motive to his question. Carefully she answered, 'I haven't seen as much of his work as you. But I think he's very able; he knows his medicine. He works hard, has a good relationship with the patients. He's confident.'

'That's only half of being a GP. What's his character like? Is he entitled to be confident?'

She didn't like these questions because she wasn't sure where Harry was leading. 'I think he is,' she said. 'He's definite, decisive. He makes up his mind on the right course of action and follows it.'

'I've noticed that. Is it a good trait for a GP?'

She thought for a moment. 'It is until you get something wrong.'

'Hmm.' After a moment he said gloomily, 'I've never supervised anyone worth millions of pounds before.'

'It's a new experience,' she agreed.

Before they could continue the conversation Micah came in, followed closely by Martin. For some reason there was none of the normal banter that was usual when they were all together. Ruth glanced at Micah. He was wearing that expression—or lack of expression—again. Her feeling of disquiet increased. She suspected she wasn't going to like what was coming.

Harry coughed, then said, 'This is going to be an

important meeting, so we'd better start. First of all, I'll explain that I've been a bit underhand. I've asked Micah to do some work that is not strictly to do with his training. But I thought he was the right man for the job. I also asked him not to mention it to you yet—until he thought he was ready.'

Ruth didn't like this at all.

'We all know that the practice can't carry on as it is,' Harry continued. 'These premises were fine twenty-five years ago, they aren't now. We're over-crowded and inefficient. So I asked Micah if he'd mind using his financial expertise to come up with a few suggestions.'

Ruth didn't know what to think. Martin smiled broadly and said, 'I'm glad you didn't ask me, Dad.'

Micah stood. For a moment Ruth thought there was a glance which asked for her understanding, but it was quickly gone.

'I hope you'll forgive me for being formal,' he said. 'And Ruth and Martin, I hope you'll forgive me for not being frank with you. I'm afraid sometimes it's the way I am.' He glanced at Ruth, who looked back at him stony-faced.

'The first thing to emphasise,' he continued, 'is that what I have to suggest is intended to provide better care for the patients. They must benefit—otherwise there's no point in changing. And I think these changes will help.'

From his briefcase he took three sets of papers and handed them round. 'I'll go through these proposals in a moment, but the next point to make is that if the practice is to change it should do so radically. Harry's just said nothing much has changed in twenty-five years. I suggest it now jumps twenty-five years into

the future. There's no point in changing a little at a
time. It must all be changed now.'

Ruth didn't know what to feel. She was seeing a
new side of Micah—and, although she wasn't sure she
liked it, reluctantly she had to admire it. The considerate doctor, the passionate lover were gone. It was
easy to see how this man—decisive, efficient, a little
brusque—had become a multimillionaire.

As he spoke she grew more and more horrified. The
changes he suggested so casually were vast!

He said that the practice should move into much
larger premises, either building them or converting an
existing building. Something called a cost/rent scheme
would enable them to do this quite cheaply. The new
building would be a complete medical centre, with
nurses, a counsellor, chiropodists, and other ancillary
staff. All their services, such as antenatal clinics, would
be brought under one roof. There would be a suite
for minor surgery. Some facilities could be rented out
to other local doctors.

He also said that they should take over Dr Parry's
patients, and a new computer system would replace
the old one they had at the moment. Everyone would
have to be retrained and they would probably need to
double or treble the number of staff.

Micah smiled at his obviously shocked audience. 'I
can see this takes some getting used to,' he said. 'But
there are two points. Firstly, Bannick needs something
like this. The patients are entitled to it. Secondly, this is
the practice style of the future. If the firm of Crowder,
Crowder and Francis doesn't introduce these reforms,
then someone else in the town will.'

Micah's next set of points lost Ruth completely. In

fact she didn't try to listen. He was explaining how this projected expansion should be financed, and as he dealt with loans, government grants and deferred mortgage payments she lost interest. With a touch of bitterness she saw that both Martin and Harry were listening intently. But she hadn't come into medicine to be an accountant. All she wanted to do was treat people.

And this wasn't medicine. And this human calculating machine wasn't Micah. She couldn't love this kind of man.

His talk was now drawing to a close. He suggested that they all study his proposals and then meet again when they had questions.

'There is one last thing,' he said. 'If you decide to go ahead with these proposals then I'll recommend someone who can help you more than I can. It might be better if I didn't have too much influence on your decisions. The reason is that you'll have to take on more doctors. And if I pass this probationary year, then I would like to buy my way into Crowder, Crowder and Francis as a junior partner.'

'We'd be very pleased to have you,' said both Harry and Martin.

Ruth didn't say anything. When Harry tried to catch her eye, she looked away.

# CHAPTER EIGHT

RUTH placed the envelope with the tickets inside on the centre of Harry's desk. 'I've made my mind up,' she said. 'They're no use to me; I've no one to go on a romantic weekend with. I'd like you and Enid to go to Paris.'

Harry scowled and pushed the envelope back towards her with his pen. 'That is nonsense. You must have a friend somewhere.'

'Must I? Who?' she asked.

Harry didn't answer for a minute. Then, without looking at her, he said, 'You won the prize when you were with Micah. I don't suppose you want to go with him?'

'This is supposed to be a romantic visit, Harry. Micah is a colleague and a friend. But we're not lovers.'

The statement wasn't quite a lie. They had been lovers—but she did not yet know what would happen in the future.

'I heard you went out with him last Wednesday.'

'Just a walk, Harry,' she said, inwardly cursing the Bannick intelligence system. 'We both needed the exercise.'

'Hmm. What did you think of his presentation?' Harry's shrewd blue eyes made her feel uncomfortable.

'A bit of a shock,' she said evasively. 'I still haven't had a chance to look through those papers he gave us.'

'We can't put off things which have got to come,' Harry said.

'I still think we're doing a pretty good job as we are.' Ruth stood. At the moment she didn't want further discussion.

'I'll put this envelope in the safe,' Harry called after her. 'I still think you should go.'

'Take Enid,' she called back, and quickly shut the door.

It had taken her quite a while to decide to offer the tickets to Harry. She'd leafed through the brochure, thrilling to the idea of walking along the Champs Elysées, visiting the Louvre. But she'd grown accustomed to making her own decisions. She would not just do what other people wanted her to.

Recently it seemed that everyone knew better than she did what the right thing for her was. She wondered if she really wanted a place in Micah's new medical palace. Perhaps she should shop round, try to find a partnership in another practice? This thought was so disagreeable that her temper grew even worse.

It wasn't a good time for Micah suddenly to appear in the corridor.

'Ruth, the very woman. Have you anything on at the moment? Could you spare me a couple of hours?'

It was the middle of the day and she only had one call to make that afternoon. Grudgingly she agreed that she could spare the time.

He didn't seem to notice her ill temper. Taking her arm, he said, 'I like little surprises. This is one for you. Come on; we have to go by car.'

'Just so long as my surprise doesn't include being

attacked by you in public in the middle of Bannick,' she said nastily.

'Ruth, would I?'

'Yes,' she said sourly, and her temper wasn't improved by his great shout of laughter.

They drove through Bannick and out to where the hill rose steeply on the northern edge of the town. After five minutes he turned off and stopped to push open gates leading into a drive. There was a small gatehouse, now derelict, and a sign saying 'Goose Hall'.

'I like the name,' he said.

They drove through parkland for a while and as they turned a corner Ruth caught sight of a house ahead. Its lines, its situation caught her interest at once though she was not about to say so. Two minutes later they pulled up outside the empty house.

In spite of her ill temper Ruth had to look at it with interest. It was shabby and had obviously been empty for quite some time. There were weeds growing in the flowerbeds, it desperately needed painting, and one or two windows were broken. But the house itself was beautiful.

Its setting was breathtaking. Sheltered by rising fields behind, in front the ground dipped away from the forecourt, showing Bannick in the valley below and the Lakeland fells in the distance.

The house wasn't too large, and was built of grey stone and slate. At first glance the lines of the Georgian building looked obvious. But as she looked Ruth realised that the pillared entrance, windows and chimneys all made one harmonious whole.

'What d'you think?' he asked.

'I think it's glorious,' she said slowly. 'And I never knew it existed. What are we doing here?'

'I've got the keys,' he said, not answering her. 'Come and look round inside. It's got lots of what estate agents call "potential". In other words, it's in a mess. But I think I like it.'

Inside they looked at the square hall, the exquisite staircase curving down into it, a dining room panelled in mahogany, elegant fireplaces, a kitchen range that was an antique. Ruth fell in love with the house and could imagine how it would look if it was decorated and furnished appropriately. But it would need a vast amount of money spent on it. The thought of money made her turn to Micah.

'You're thinking of buying this place, aren't you?'

He nodded. 'I think it's what I've always wanted. A beautiful house with land and roots in the past. They make me feel very comfortable at the Bell but it reminds me that never in my life have I had a place I could call my own. In London I lived in digs and then service flats. All very luxurious—but not home.'

'Why did you bring me to see it?'

He looked at her keenly. 'I value your opinion. I thought you would be interested—perhaps in time very interested. You've made your house into a home; you could help me get the same effect here.'

She laughed without humour. 'There's just a bit of difference in size.'

It had been a mistake for him to refer to her cottage. As she thought of it, it became a refuge. *Her* home designed to make *her* comfortable, where she could live with her memories free of other people interfering with her life.

Now he was pointing to the fields around them, studded with trees and sheep. 'The house comes on its own or with all the land around, which is leased to a local farmer. I'd buy the land to make sure no one built nearby.'

'What about the farmer?' she asked savagely.

'I hope he'd carry on leasing the land. I'd offer it at the same rent.'

The gentle answer did nothing to soften her anger. Now she was angry at herself for being angry. She didn't know what she wanted.

'Ruth, come here and sit down.' They had entered a shelf-lined study. Fitted into the window alcove was a seat where you could sit and gaze down across the valley. He sat in one corner, and reluctantly she squeezed herself into the other.

'Let's play doctors and patients,' he said, smiling. 'And I'll be doctor to start. Since we got here your behaviour has been odd. Your body language suggests you're resisting something—or someone. Your arms are folded tightly, you're avoiding eye contact, and even now you're pressed against that wall. What's wrong?'

She realised he was right. Her body was tense—but she didn't need him to tell her that. Consciously she made an effort to relax. Then she felt a flash of irritation as she caught his half-hidden smile. He'd recognised what she was doing.

'I do like the house,' she said, avoiding his main question. 'And with some work you should be able to make it look really beautiful. I hope you'll invite me to visit when it's finished.' She tried an insincere smile.

Suddenly his hands shot forward and grabbed her

just above her elbows. He shook her, but gently, as she jerked back from him. 'Ruth, what is this? This is me, Micah, talking. You know, the man you. . . walked on the moors with.'

'Walking's a new word for it,' she muttered and he smiled.

'That's better. I like it when you fight back. You're human now. For the last hour you've been acting as if you were on another planet.'

'Perhaps that's the way I want it to be. Can't you leave it at that?'

He shook his head. 'No, I can't. I want to know.'

She recognised the steel in his voice, the determination to get an answer no matter what it cost. She'd come across this quality before. Her dead husband Matt had had it. It wasn't a good time for her to remember.

'Give me a minute,' she said. 'I need just a bit longer.'

For a moment he stared at her keenly and then he said, 'Of course. Look, I left a torch in the car. I'll fetch it and we can explore in the attics. I've been fascinated by attics since I was a child.'

'All right,' she said. She didn't tell him that she had always felt the same.

From the first floor they climbed a much steeper staircase at the back of the house. They found a complete set of rooms with low ceilings, presumably once the home of the servants. Four had tiny round windows, two were dark, little more than alcoves under the eaves. As Micah swung the torch round Ruth caught his arm. 'What's that—up in the corner?'

He shone the light where she pointed. A wooden

beam supported the sloping wall and where it neared the ceiling there was some kind of mark.

He fetched an old stool from the landing and stood on it to brush away the cobwebs. Then he stared at what he'd revealed.

'What's it say?' she asked.

He didn't answer, but stepped down, handed her the torch and steadied her as she climbed onto the stool. She was intensely aware of his hand on her waist but forced her attention on the beam. There was a carving, much painted over but still very clear. It had been cut deep into the wood, obviously with care. A heart had two names above it—Tom and Irene. Below it said 'Love for ever—1912'.

With the tip of her finger she traced the outline of the heart. 'Love for ever in 1912,' she said. 'I wonder if it was? I remember someone telling me that by 1918 over half the young men in Bannick had been killed in France. I wonder if Tom was one of them?'

He pulled her gently from the stool. 'They still had two years,' he said, 'and two years is better than nothing. Come on; the sun's shining outside. Let's go and walk in the garden.'

He took her outside where to one side of the house there was a walled garden. Old fruit trees and bushes now ran riot over the decorative tiled footpaths, but Ruth could see how little work it would need to restore it to the magic place it had obviously once been. She forced herself not to think of it, not to plan. She would never have anything to do with this garden.

As they walked Micah held her hand. She didn't object, but let her own hand rest in his, lifeless.

'It's nice out here,' he said, 'but you look grim. You don't smile and there are shadows under your eyes.'

'I'm sorry if my appearance doesn't meet with your approval.'

'You look how you always look, Ruth: gorgeous.' Her lips twitched a little at the extravagant compliment.

He went on, 'Perhaps you need a holiday. How long since you had one?'

'Are you thinking of a romantic weekend for two? I gave Harry the tickets this morning.'

'Now that's a pity! I'd hoped you could have taken me.'

Flatly she said, 'There was no chance. Bannick Travel Agency is run by Lewis Somers. He's a nice, helpful fellow, but if I'd taken you everyone in Bannick would have known inside a week.'

'Would it have mattered?'

'It would matter to me. I have to live here.'

After a pause he said, 'I was hoping—am hoping— to live here too.'

They came to a stand of ancient roses, thick and unpruned, growing in a tangle to arch over their heads. She stopped to pull one of the great yellow flowers towards her and smell its scent. When she let the flower go a thorn caught her and she winced. A tiny drop of blood grew on the tip of her finger.

He took her hand and raised it to his lips. 'I'll kiss it better,' he said.

'Like in a fairy story? Remember the sleeping beauty—after one prick she slept for a hundred years.'

'Ruth, don't play games; I want to talk to you. I want to be honest with you.' Abruptly, his previous impish mood had seemed to desert him. Ruth wondered if at last she'd pierced that tough outer layer that made him so difficult to hurt.

He smiled sourly. 'In the money market, whenever anyone used the word "honest" it was supposed to be a certain sign that they were about to lie. Well, I'm not.'

He took a deep breath. 'I'm new to this area and I love it. I'm new to the job and I love that too. And I've met you. I'm not now going to say I love you, though a large part of me wants to. But I'm getting that way. I like your sense of humour, I like working with you, I like being with you. When we were on the mountain it was something else—and it was for you too, wasn't it?'

Ruth couldn't say anything. She could only nod dumbly.

He went on, 'I want a long-term relationship and I've never had one before. We've got to go forward and I can't do it alone. You can't put something like this on hold. It isn't something you can put down and pick up weeks later. We need commitment from both sides. Ruth, do you hear what I'm saying?'

'I hear what you're saying,' she dragged out, 'but I don't know that I want to answer.'

She heard his breathing, lifted her bowed head to see his face. It was hard and humourless. She knew how much she'd affected him.

'I must have time, Micah,' she said. 'You've got to give me time. I've been happy with my life for years now and you're trying to turn it upside down.'

'You're always asking for time! And I think you've already turned my life upside down!'

When she said nothing he smiled resignedly. 'Come on. Perhaps we ought to get back to work.'

She followed him in silence.

Her one call that afternoon was to see Gail Thompson's mother. To Ruth's surprise Mrs Thompson seemed quite pleased to see her. She insisted on pouring Ruth a cup of tea; this was an olive branch. But as the woman talked Ruth became anxious and angry. She knew that Micah had come to talk to the family. She hadn't realised what he had done. And she knew how persuasive Micah could be.

'So what did Dr North suggest?' she asked the almost talkative woman.

'Well, he was very good. He reminded me what it was like when I had my own family—how they were trouble at first but afterwards how you couldn't be parted from them. And he said that Mr Smart was really sorry for what his son had done—I ought to give him a little credit for that, and it would be doing him a favour to accept something from him. Not that he needs any favours! And Dr North went to see my husband in hospital and the two of them got along just fine. So it's more or less arranged.'

'What is arranged?' asked Ruth warily.

'Well, Gail will keep the baby. And after three or four months it can go and spend most of its time with Mrs Smart, and Gail can go back to college. Apparently Mrs Smart always wanted more babies and she wants to bring this one up.'

Ruth didn't believe this. 'What do social services think?'

Mrs Thompson shrugged. 'They can think what they

like—not that we're going to tell them. As Dr North says, who we pick as babysitters is our affair.'

'And Gail is quite happy about this?'

Mrs Thompson nodded. 'Very happy.'

'You've taken a very big and brave decision. Was it easy?'

'When we thought it through it was obvious. And Dr North helped us to see that there were alternatives we hadn't thought of.'

'I'm sure he did,' said Ruth, and stood up to leave. 'I'll see Gail in surgery soon.'

'He's very understanding, that Dr North,' Mrs Thompson called after her.

Ruth forced a brittle smile. 'He's made a big impression on us,' she said.

She caught Micah in the corridor, just before evening surgery. 'I've been to Gail Thompson's house,' she said curtly. 'Apparently you've been quite busy there. You've talked them into keeping the baby so that Mrs Smart can have it as her own child.'

He stood and thought for a moment. 'I think that's a bit slick—but I suppose it's more or less correct.'

'Micah, do you know what you've done? You've interfered with other people's lives. You've pushed them into doing things they wouldn't have done themselves. You've played God.'

'I don't think so. Perhaps I've helped things along a bit, but I think it's a solution that should benefit everybody—especially the baby.'

'It's not our job! Being a doctor is dangerous; people can get to think you can cure all problems. All we should cure is illness.'

He shook his head slowly. 'We deal with people, not illnesses. I think there's a scale. We can interfere in people's lives; we can help them or we just treat symptoms and ignore what we know is really wrong because it's not our job. You've accused me of interfering and I know I've taken a chance. But I thought about it. And I believe I've done what's best for everyone.'

There was a loud cough behind them. Mary was signalling that there were people waiting; doctors should be in their consulting rooms, not gossiping in the corridor.

'I hope you're not proved wrong,' Ruth whispered angrily, and disappeared into her room.

She drove home after surgery, bathed and changed into a tracksuit. She cooked and ate something—next day she couldn't remember what. Then she sat on her settee and told herself that she would not move until she had decided what to do about Micah.

She couldn't start. Her mind refused to face the stark choices in front of her. Then, as her eyes flashed round her living room, seeking some escape, they lit upon the picture of Matt. Here would be her beginning.

She had fallen in love—or rather she'd been dragged into love. Matt Francis had done everything in a hurry, never thinking of the consequences. She had wanted to wait till they both qualified, but he had insisted they get married at once. She had loved him and she had known he loved her. But now, with the wisdom of experience, she realised that she had not been entirely happy. Life had been too much of a tumult. She couldn't go through that again.

So what about Micah? Too much of him was like

her ex-husband. He too took risks—though he called it making decisions. They had made love on the mountaintop and she knew it was an experience she'd never forget. She had felt alive, complete; there had been an ecstasy in giving as well as receiving. But that kind of joy could be taken away. She couldn't bear to lose again.

Until a few weeks ago she'd been perfectly happy. To herself she repeated the self-comforting words she thought so often. I am Dr Ruth Francis. I am contented, successful, well respected. I need nothing more than what I have now. The words throbbed through her head. She just couldn't stand more upheaval. Her affair with Dr Micah North would have to end. She would tell him tomorrow.

For an hour she sat motionless in her chair. Her decision had now been made, and she knew she was tough enough to carry it through. But the prospect of life ahead seemed grey.

Next morning she was in luck—if that was the right word for it. She drove into the car park immediately behind Micah's Range Rover. She had wondered how and when to tell him; it struck her that this bleak time would be as good as any.

He smiled at her, then looked quizzical as he registered the coldness of her voice.

'Micah, could I have a word? It won't take a minute.'

'You may have as long as you wish,' he said urbanely.

It would be best to be quick and cold. She didn't want to hurt him—or herself, she realised.

'I've been thinking about us—and what you said

yesterday. It's no good, Micah. We can be colleagues and friends, I hope, but never anything more.'

She'd said it and it hurt.

He looked at her assessingly. 'Do we have to deal with our lives in a car park? Can't we discuss this somewhere?'

'There's nothing to discuss. I've thought about it. I've made my decision. Please don't bring the subject up again.'

His face was grim, but he said nothing. Falteringly she went on, 'I know I've probably been at fault, leading you on. But it wasn't deliberate. I can only say I'm sorry.'

'I'm sorry too, Ruth. I'll respect your wishes of course, but—'

'Morning! Another glorious day!'

They turned. Behind them was Harry, beaming face at the open window of his car, carefully reversing in beside them. Ruth looked up. It *was* a glorious day. So far she hadn't noticed.

'Good morning, Harry,' she called, then turned back to Micah. 'I don't think there's anything else to say,' she said pleasantly. 'Let's consider the matter closed.'

'As you wish.'

The three of them walked towards the surgery front door. Ruth had been dreading the conversation she'd just had. Now that it was over she wondered why she didn't feel any sense of relief.

Cheerfully Harry said, 'Ruth, I'd like you to meet Janet Williams. She's going to subject us all to an expert examination, financial and procedural, over the next week.'

It was their usual casual lunchtime meeting. Harry, Martin and Micah were already drinking coffee. Ruth had forgotten that Micah had promised to find someone who could advise them on the most efficient way of altering the practice. And she certainly hadn't expected anyone like this smart young woman.

'Hello, Dr Francis; I'm very pleased to meet you,' said Janet Williams. 'I hope not to interfere in your work at all.'

Ruth shook the outstretched hand, her smile of welcome absolutely genuine. Janet was slim and small, but wearing heels to give her height. Her hair was a thick black cap, its simplicity suggesting expensive cutting. Her make-up was flawless, her grey summer dress was silk. And Janet had the broadest Welsh accent Ruth had ever heard.

'Please call me Ruth,' she said. 'I hope you enjoy your stay with us.'

'Since we're all here,' Harry said, 'it might be a good idea to explain what's happening. At present Janet's here almost unofficially, staying at the Bell as Micah's guest. She's supposed to be on holiday. After two or three days she'll give us a preliminary report. If we're interested in going further, then we'll put things on a more formal basis. Janet?'

Janet pulled forward a laptop computer and tapped it. 'I need to get something in here. This morning I'd like to get some background facts and a general feel for the practice. This afternoon and tomorrow I'd like to look through the accounts for the past five years. I've arranged to speak to Dr Parry on Wednesday morning. I shall also have a word with a couple of estate agents and perhaps visit other possible premises.

'If, after a preliminary report, you're interested, then I suggest that one or two of you visit practices I've helped set up in the past year. I can arrange this. Then I'd like you to retain me officially. I would no longer be Micah's friend, but have a professional responsibility to the practice itself.'

Ruth blinked. She could see that Harry and Martin were also taken aback. The doll-like Welsh girl in the pretty frock had suddenly turned into a dynamic businesswoman. Only Micah appeared unsurprised, and Ruth realised why. Janet Williams was like him. They both moved easily in this financial world of cool, exact decisions. It was foreign to Ruth.

Janet had something else to say. 'One last thing. I believe the only purpose of reorganisation is to benefit your patients. I'm going to have little to do with the medical side of things but I've got it on my mind all the time. Thank you.'

Janet was—bracing. Ruth felt that listening to her was like walking for an hour against a high wind. She accepted a cup of coffee from Martin and turned to sit down. The only free seat was next to Micah.

It was a week now since she'd told him that their affair was over. Over? she thought. It had barely begun.

To the rest of the practice there was no change in their relationship; they were still friends and colleagues, conferring at times, sharing jokes in Harry's room. But Ruth could tell there was anger and hurt behind those green eyes. He'd never said anything to her but she knew what he was feeling by the way he sometimes looked at her. In the corridor or checking something in the library he would glance at her, and that glance would sear her soul.

She felt numb. She carried on with her job but she took no joy in it. All she could do was work on, and hope that in time some contentment would creep back into the greyness of her existence. But could she ever hope for contentment when Micah was so close? His very presence hurt her.

She turned to him and smiled. 'Janet seems very efficient,' she said quietly. 'We're lucky to have her.'

'I thought you weren't very keen on change, Ruth?'

She shrugged. 'We all have to move on sometimes. Perhaps I've been stuck in the mud for too long.'

'Perhaps.'

It was only one word, spoken perfectly politely, but as he looked at her there was an instant of communication. She could sense the pain he was feeling and suspected that he could read the same in her eyes. She knew she had to leave the room at once.

'Nice to meet you, Janet,' she called across the room. 'Good luck with the research. Afraid I have to dash.' Grabbing her bag, she walked out of the room, leaving her coffee half-drunk. Life was getting too hard!

She kept out of Micah's way over the next few days but she seemed to run into Janet Williams quite often. At first she'd been prepared to dislike the girl, but after a while she found her friendly and re-freshingly earthy. Janet had a drive and enthusiasm for her work that Ruth remembered once having herself.

She'd also half expected to be jealous. There was no need. It was very obvious that there was nothing sexual between Janet and Micah. What there was was something more subtle. Janet represented the call of

the business world, and Ruth wondered if Micah still
hankered after it.

What should she do herself? Did she really want
to be part of this new, super-efficient practice?
The thought of having to move was too dismaying.
But she certainly couldn't stay on with Micah. Then,
on Friday morning, Janet invited her to lunch at
the Bell.

'I know we've had little conversations in corners,'
she said cheerfully, 'but I'd like to have a longer talk.
Perhaps I can persuade you that this change isn't all
bad news.'

'I've never said it was bad news,' Ruth protested.

Janet winked. 'But that's what you think. It's a reaction I've come across before. I'm afraid it's a bit
obvious.'

'Oh, dear,' Ruth said flatly. She'd thought she'd kept
her views well hidden.

The lunch was a success. At Janet's request Ruth had
arranged to have much of the afternoon free. They sat
in a window-seat and ate grilled trout and salad, with
a bottle of Saumur. Outside, people caught Ruth's eye
and she seemed constantly to be waving through the
window. Janet watched this with amusement.

'You seem to know everybody in town,' she said.

'Certainly a fair number. I was born, bred and I
practise here.'

'You're lucky. I know hardly anyone in London and
I've lived there years. Shall we have coffee in the
lounge?'

After three-quarters of an hour's discussion and
explanation Ruth was beginning to think that perhaps

she was wrong. The changes Janet was to suggest *would* benefit patients. But it would be a new way of life, and she wasn't looking forward to it.

Seeing that she had made an impression, Janet cleverly changed the subject to something more personal.

'You're lucky to have Micah North,' she said casually. 'Are you interested in him, Ruth?'

Ruth felt her face grow slightly warm. 'You mean—er—sexually?' she asked. 'No, I'm not at all. But I like him and I think he'll make a good doctor.'

Janet looked at her but said nothing and Ruth remembered how astute she was. 'In fact I thought it was you two who were lovers,' she said. 'And that you'd come up here just to be with him.'

Janet smiled. 'I hope ultimately to profit by my trip. But you're right. I would have come just for him. He did me a big favour some years ago and I'll never forget it.'

'What kind of favour?' Ruth found a bitter-sweet pleasure in talking about Micah. Besides, she wanted to know what he had been like when he'd lived in London. She knew little of his life before he'd come here.

'I was a young trader and I bought too much of something. Then I was stuck with it. One mistake, but it could have been the end of my career. Micah bought the stock from me—he was big enough to ride the loss for a week or so. Of all the people to help me, I was surprised it was Micah North.

'Anyway, he got really angry with me and gave me an unmerciful telling-off; I remember it to this day. We were in the middle of a pavement in the City and it was raining. He wouldn't even let me go in out of the rain.'

Janet grinned mischievously. 'I had a white silk blouse on. It got soaked through and I wasn't wearing a bra. So there he was, shouting at a woman who was in effect naked from the waist up, and he didn't even notice. When he finished he lent me his jacket.'

'What did he say to you?' asked Ruth. She was fascinated by this insight into Micah's character— though she found it very believable.

'He told me always to ask if I didn't know. Then he said that a trader should always know the difference between stupid risks and necessary ones.'

'Did he? I've heard him say something like that to me.' Ruth knew she'd have to think about this. She went on, 'And you say you've never really fancied him?'

'Well, who wouldn't fancy him? But in my case it was only from a distance. He used to be very unapproachable. And anyway, don't laugh, but I'm going to marry the headmaster of a school for children with special needs. Nothing to do with money.'

Ruth thought back over what she'd just heard. There was something. . . 'You said you were surprised that Micah of all people should help you. Why?'

Janet paused to drink her coffee. Then she said, 'I shouldn't gossip about my friends. But I'll tell you this because I didn't believe you when you said you weren't interested in Micah.'

'I don't—' Ruth said but Janet interrupted her.

'If I'm wrong then I'm wrong. Sorry. Anyway, Micah helped another girl long before me—like me, another trader. For a while they were inseparable and people said the hard man was softening. He was obviously in love with her and she seemed to be in love with him. They were just about to get engaged when she apparently got a better offer. She promptly ditched Micah and went to America with a multimillionaire.'

Janet smiled as she leaned over to pour herself more coffee, well aware of Ruth's fascination with her story. She went on, 'The trading floor's a tough place, you know. Micah took some ribbing about his lost love. It was hard to tell, but I think he took some time to get over it. It didn't affect his work. If anything, he became harder than ever. He took chances, but he worked them out first. And he always said when he was ready he'd get out. Mind you, we all do that. But he said it and meant it and did it.'

'I must be getting back to the surgery,' Ruth said slowly. 'Thanks for the lunch and the chat, Janet— I've really enjoyed both.'

'Me too,' Janet said briskly. 'I hope I've given you plenty to think about.'

'Yes. There's a lot in what you say about reorganising the practice.'

'What on earth else could we have talked about?' Janet asked.

Ruth blushed as she looked into Janet's laughing eyes. This girl was shrewd.

There weren't usually many cars in the practice car park in the afternoon. But today Ruth had difficulty getting in. A vast black Rolls-Royce blocked her way until the obliging chauffeur drove forward to let her pass. Who did they know with a chauffeured car like that?

In Reception she leaned over and whispered to an intrigued Mary, 'Whose is the car?'

'It's Lord Dallan. Says he just dropped by, wondered if he could have a word with Dr North if it wasn't inconvenient. Well, it was, but he's having one anyway.'

'He's not going to sign on with us, is he?' Ruth suppressed a laugh.

'He could. . .' But as they looked down the corridor the door to Micah's room opened and Lord Dallan walked out. He turned to shake Micah's hand, said he was looking forward to hearing from him, and strode down the corridor, smiling courteously at Mary and Ruth. Micah came to join them as they watched the Rolls drive off.

'That's the trouble with the aristocracy,' Micah whispered. 'Too much crusted port leads to prostate trouble.'

Ruth smiled. She'd forgotten how witty Micah could be. 'What *did* he want?' she asked.

'Come and have a cup of tea and I'll tell you all.'

Luckily Martin and Harry were already drinking. Micah wanted to ask everyone's advice. 'Lord Dallan's just called,' he said, pouring himself and Ruth some tea. 'Apparently he's the chairman of the board of trustees of a big hospital trust in Yorkshire. There's been a lot of trouble and they're about to sack the director. Now they want someone with medical as well as financial experience. Lord Dallan came to ask me if I'd care to apply for the post.'

'You mean he offered it to you,' Ruth said.

Micah sipped his tea. 'I suppose so,' he agreed.

'And do you want to go?'

He shrugged. 'It would certainly be an interesting job. I think I could do it and it would be a job worth doing. I don't know. What do you think, Harry?'

'It's certainly a job that needs doing. Too many hospital trusts are run by people with no medical sympathies at all.'

'Hmm. It's not what I'd planned for myself. But I promised him I'd think about it.'

Quietly Ruth said, 'I think it would be a great pity. You're a good GP and I don't think that you'd be happy now just dealing with figures. There's much more to medicine than money.'

To her surprise she found that her voice was trembling slightly. She felt raw anger welling inside her. She just didn't want Micah to leave. The realisation shocked her. What should she do now?

# CHAPTER NINE

NEXT morning Ruth woke early. There was only a sheet covering her but she felt hot and sticky. When she looked out of the window she knew why. The sun was hidden in haze and there was a dirty yellow tinge to the sky. She didn't need to listen to the weather forecast. Every Bannick resident knew there was going to be a storm.

She put a mackintosh and hat handy, then dressed in the briefest of underwear and a sleeveless light blue cotton dress. Even so, she felt the slight prickle of perspiration as she walked out of her door.

At the car she stopped irresolutely for a moment, then walked back to her cottage to pick up boots and socks, a tracksuit and anorak. It was as well to be prepared for anything.

Morning surgery was a pain. The heat and humidity affected everybody; small troubles became magnified into major problems. Ruth spent as much time calming people down as she did diagnosing and prescribing. She wondered if her patients realised that doctors were human; she felt uncomfortable and bad-tempered too.

After an hour she slipped out to get herself a glass of iced water. Her temper wasn't improved by the sight of Micah, immaculate in a lightweight grey suit, apparently unaffected by the heat. He's not human, she muttered to herself.

Ruth quailed when she saw that her next patient

was Gail Thompson. She knew just how stressful this kind of weather could be to a pregnant girl and Gail hadn't shown many signs of fortitude so far.

'Come in, Gail,' she said brightly as the door opened. 'You're looking well.' To her slight surprise this statement was true.

Gail's pregnancy was now quite obvious. She was wearing an attractive multicoloured shift, her hair had been styled and she wore just a little make-up.

With a shy smile she lowered herself into the proffered chair. 'I don't think there's anything really wrong with me,' she explained, 'but I've been having these pains. My mum says I ought to expect them but. . .'

'We'll have a look at you in a minute. How's your diet? Are you following the sheet Nurse Mathers gave you?'

'Oh, yes. And my mum makes sure I get all my vitamin pills and things like that.'

'Ah,' said Ruth delicately. 'And how is your mum. . .taking things?'

'She's a lot better now. She won't see Mr Smart yet but she's talked to him on the phone. She'll see him in time.'

'I'm glad things are working out. Now come and lie down on this couch and we'll have a quick look at you.'

Ruth checked Gail's pulse and blood pressure and gently felt her rounded abdomen. All was perfectly normal. What was surprising was that Gail lay placidly through it all. Ruth remembered the last time she'd examined her, after the incident in the antenatal clinic. Gail had fidgeted, wriggled, complained, making the examination far more uncomfortable than it need have been.

'Right, Gail, you can get up now. You and your baby are perfectly healthy. Tell me what's worrying you.'

'It's just these pains, down there. . .'

Ruth had guessed what the trouble was. They were Braxton-Hicks contractions of the uterus. She explained to Gail that her body was just getting used to the idea of producing a baby. The pains were quite normal and nothing to worry about. Gail seemed relieved.

'Thanks, Dr Francis.' Gail stood to leave. 'Actually, I came here to thank you as well. You and Dr North have really sorted things out. My mum and dad are a lot happier and I suppose I am too.'

'You're welcome, Gail. I'm sure everything will work out well.' Ruth took trouble to make sure that the grimness she felt didn't show in her voice.

She showed Gail out, then sat at her desk for a moment before ringing for her next patient. She and Dr North had really sorted things out! Deliberately Ruth forced herself not to get angry. It was Micah's doing, not hers; she wanted nothing to do with this kind of interference. And yet. . .Gail had been happier. This fact made Ruth angrier than ever. What was she going to do about Micah? The cool voice of sanity spoke to her. In this heat, nothing.

At half past eleven it got suddenly dark and Ruth had to turn on her desk light. Then there was the sound of wind shaking the branches of the trees outside. She reached for a cardigan as there was a definite drop in temperature.

At first it sounded like pebbles being thrown at the window. She looked up to see the first great drops bouncing off the glass. There was a sudden roar as the rain lashed down. Ruth smiled to herself. This was the Bannick weather that the tourist board didn't advertise.

By the time Ruth joined Harry for her lunchtime coffee the rain had moderated. In place of the initial torrent there was now a hard, steady fall that seemed as if it would go on for ever. She squinted up at the sky. Not a break in sight.

'I thought they only had monsoons in the Tropics.' It was Micah; he'd entered the room behind her. As ever, the sound of that dark brown voice sent shivers down her spine. She wondered if she'd ever stop being enthralled by it.

Harry laughed. 'So speaks the effete southerner. We get a day like this every two or three years, Micah. It won't break for another twenty-four hours and there'll be all sorts of trouble. The good thing is that people will sit at home rather than come out to bother their GP.'

'I've never seen rain like it.' Micah stood by the window, fascinated.

Ruth had intended to make three distant calls out on the moors that afternoon, but none was urgent so she rang to cancel. Everyone she spoke to agreed that it was a good idea. Millie Carson said that Ruth wouldn't get up the road without a tractor anyway.

As Ruth had expected, evening surgery was very sparsely attended. Only she and Micah were on duty and neither had many patients. Ruth almost found herself extending consultations to keep from being bored. The rain continued its inexorable downpour.

Then, at six o'clock, just as she finished writing a prescription, Mary rang through. 'It's Sergeant Black on the line. He says it's an emergency.'

Ruth glanced at the rain drumming on her window and winced. She didn't like emergencies at all, though she'd dealt with many. She quickly ushered her patient out. 'Put him on, Mary.'

The members of her practice had a friendly relationship with the police. In a small town like Bannick they often found themselves having to work together. And Roger Black was one of the many people she knew from her schooldays.

'Dr Francis? Sergeant Black here.' Ruth felt a chill run down her spine. She didn't like the formality; it was usually Ruth and Roger.

'Can I help you, Roger?' she asked. She wasn't going to call him Sergeant Black.

'We have a problem, Ruth. I don't yet know how big. And this rain's got all the emergency services out. We've got a big pile-up on the motorway and the mountain rescue team's thirty miles away helping three fallen climbers. I'm short of men.'

At the words 'mountain rescue team' Ruth's heart had started to beat faster, but she managed to sound calm. 'What d'you want us to do?'

'We've just had a call. A school minibus was coming from the top of Lexton Hill. You know that little track? Well, the road's washed away again and the bus slid down the hill and turned over. There's no way I can get an ambulance up there. We can get a Land Rover to about a quarter of a mile away. I've sent one and I'm going in the next.'

'How badly are people injured?' Ruth rapped out.

'We don't know yet. Report is of the driver trapped under the bus but the kids are all alive. We won't know till we get there. All we've got so far is a message from a half-hysterical woman on one of those portable phones. And the signal keeps breaking up. I'll know better when my lads get there.'

She felt sick at the idea of an overturned bus, young bodies injured in this evil weather and no way of getting them to hospital. And Lexton Hill was close to Ironstone Edge where her husband had been. . .

She shook herself; she was a doctor. Still holding the phone, she walked to the large-scale map pinned to her wall. She knew Lexton Hill well. She saw the route from the summit to where she knew the road would have given way, where the contours were closest. It had happened before.

Her fingers traced the road's path then dropped to the valley below to where there was a tiny stream marked, and a single black square.

'Thought so.' She smiled with satisfaction. 'Roger, there's a walkers' hut in the valley about three hundred yards from the crash. It belongs to a group called the Northern Moors Fellowship. I've been in it; there'll be some food and blankets and something to burn. You'll find a key under the water butt at the back.'

'You want us to set up a first-stage medical post?'

'If you can't get ambulances there, then yes. There's nothing else to do in this weather. My partner will drive me there along the valley floor; he's got a Range Rover.'

'We'll see you there, Doctor.' Roger rang off.

It wasn't the time for hasty action. For a moment she sat at her desk and mentally ran through everything she needed, everything that had to be done. Then she went to see Mary.

'There's been an accident out at Lexton Hill, Mary. I'm going with Dr North.'

This kind of thing had happened before, if not very often. Mary merely nodded and said she would cancel what she could and phone to let Martin and Harry know. She'd stay in Reception till relieved.

Ruth rang through to Micah. 'We have an emergency—an accident out on the moors. Will you drive me there?'

'What do we need to take?' His voice was perfectly controlled. Even at a time like this Ruth had to admire him.

'I'm the local doctor the police call out in cases like this. There's a special emergency pack in the back of my car.'

Outside the rain was as heavy as ever. Micah helped her carry the heavy emergency boxes and heaved them into the back of his Range Rover. With her mac over her head Ruth went back to her car and grabbed the clothes she'd thrown in earlier. She was going to need them.

Micah drove the great car through the town centre, now almost deserted. There was the constant drumming of rain on the roof and from their front wheels two hissing waves of water splashed. Ruth directed him onto a narrow country road that twisted up into the hills.

'This is something completely new to me, Ruth. Is there any set procedure, anything I should know?'

She glanced at him sideways. He was still in his light grey suit, but with a mac thrown over it. It had done little to protect him from the rain; his face was wet and the thick dark hair was bedraggled and hung over his forehead. Some stray part of her mind registered that even in this state he was the most captivating man she'd ever met. She thrust the thought aside.

'We're a kind of last line of defence—to be called out when ambulances are delayed or something.' She explained why the ambulances couldn't get through. Then she went on, 'We're setting up a first-stage medical post. Think of it as a battlefield. We're not practising medicine so much as first aid. What we've got to do is make sure nobody actually gets worse until they can have proper medical attention.'

'So no appendectomies with a tin-opener?'

The joke bewildered her for a moment. Then she realised what he was doing. She was sounding stressed, a little too much on edge. He wanted to calm her. 'Only if it's a sharp one,' she quipped back, and he turned to smile at her.

Even though she was wearing her mac, the rain had half soaked her thin light blue dress. She grimaced. It would be a positive hindrance when they got to the hut. First she checked that the clothes she'd thrown in were within easy reach. Then she kicked off her sandals, reached down to the hem of her dress and, with a wriggle, pulled it over her head. She dropped it behind her seat and sat for a moment in the lacy white bra and briefest of briefs. She felt she had to dress a little sedately for the practice, but she always treated herself to ultra-feminine underwear.

'This may be entirely the wrong time to say this, but once again, Dr Francis, you look gorgeous.'

'I wish I had something a little more substantial,' she muttered, but she felt a guilty glow of pleasure

at the compliment. She quickly scrambled into her
tracksuit, anorak and boots.

Following her instructions, he turned the Range
Rover off the narrow road and they bumped down a
farm track, now almost entirely obliterated by running
water. After a moment Micah stopped and engaged
the differential lock. Ahead, showing grey in the murk,
they could see the dim outline of Lexton Hill.

The farm track ended and ahead of them was a
stream, thick with mud and now three times its normal
width. Ruth gazed at it in horror. It looked dangerous.

'There is an actual path,' she said, 'on the left
bank of this stream. Unfortunately the bank is under
water.'

'I think we can get through.' The car lurched down
onto the path and plunged wheel-deep into the water.
She reminded herself that he'd been on a course in
this kind of driving.

It was slow work but they were moving. The mass
of Lexton Hill grew closer and they entered a little
ravine. Uneasily she looked at the steep, rocky walls
growing closer on each side. In spite of the car, in
spite of Micah's presence beside her, she suddenly felt
a frightening sense of claustrophobia.

This wasn't an accident, it was a mountain rescue.
Like the time when her husband had died. A sound,
half sob, half groan, burst from her lips. She was afraid!

'Ruth! What's the matter?' After a pause he went
on, 'You're thinking of your husband, aren't you?'

She couldn't reply. Visions from the past came back
to haunt her: the empty house, the nervous policeman
and woman who had come to tell her that they had
'some bad news' for her.

'You're thinking of his death, aren't you?
Answer me!'

Now he sounded angry and she managed to speak.
'It just all came back to me. It. . .it wasn't far from
here that it happened.'

His voice was cold and curt. 'That is now in the
past. You are a doctor; you have patients waiting.
They are young, cold, frightened, possibly injured.
They need reassurance and competence from you. So
pull yourself together!'

The last four words were shouted and she jerked in
her seat. Then he added in a totally different voice,
'Pretend you're a pair of curtains.'

There was silence for a moment. Then she took a
deep breath and said, 'I think that's the worst joke
I've ever heard. But it's worked. I'm all right now;
don't worry about me.'

'I do,' was the brief reply.

'There are times when you're good for me,' she said,
knowing she meant it. Before he could answer she
went on, 'Just round that rocky corner is the hut. The
front door's on the other side.'

'Time to start work.'

The Northern Moors Fellowship hut looked dark
and forbidding in the lashing rain. The shutters
were still up but there seemed to be smoke trying to
escape from the chimney. The car pulled up outside.
Ruth ran to the front door as Micah fetched her
emergency kit.

She took in the scene inside at once. Eight children,
aged eleven or twelve, wrapped in blankets, huddled
close to a fire. Some had bloody pads which they
clutched to head or arm. A young policewoman—girl,

in fact—was looking doubtfully at a bandage which she was pressing to the face of an older woman who was obviously in pain and distress.

The policewoman's relief at seeing Ruth was unmistakable. 'Dr Francis, isn't it? I'm glad you're here. We've lit the fire and I've done what I can for the kids but this is Miss Fawcett and she's—'

'I think you've done a great job. . .what's your name?'

'WPC Walker, Doctor—Angela Walker.'

'Right, Angela, help me get Miss Fawcett into the back room. There's a bunk there we can use.' Ruth knew that an upset senior woman would only disturb the children.

'Please,' said Miss Fawcett in a strange, high-pitched voice, 'it's poor Mr Moody; he's trapped under the van. I got the children out of a window and took them some distance away as you should, and I rang for the police, but Mr Moody was screaming and I don't know what the headmaster will say. I. . .'

Ruth recognised the signs of hysteria. She tried to speak calmly and comfortingly as she said, 'Miss Fawcett, you've done everything really well. The police and the doctor will see to Mr Moody. Soon we'll have you in hospital and I know the headmaster will be delighted with you.'

The door banged open and Micah strode in with the emergency box. Quickly Ruth said, 'Triage on the children first, Micah, then come and help me with Miss Fawcett here.'

'OK. Shout if I'm needed urgently.' As Ruth gently coaxed Miss Fawcett into the back room she heard Micah say, 'Right, one at a time. And when we've had a quick look at you then we'll eat. You all look ravenous.'

Ruth closed the door and turned to her patient. She was a middle-aged woman with sensible glasses and neat grey hair, now dishevelled. As Ruth eased the blanket from round her shoulders she saw mud-stained sweater, trousers and boots that all shouted 'teacher'. Miss Fawcett was clutching her arm and winced as Ruth touched it.

'It will be all right, won't it?' she asked.

'Of course,' soothed Ruth. 'You've done wonderfully well so far. Angela, could you help me take off this sweater?'

Miss Fawcett's pulse was quick and thready, but she looked the healthy type and Ruth guessed she was resilient. After a quick look at the pad Angela was holding to Miss Fawcett's face, Ruth reached for a pressure bandage. The bleeding was quite serious; she'd have to come back to it.

The initial adrenalin surge would hold back the pain, but Ruth guessed that it would shortly get worse. She swabbed Miss Fawcett's arm and injected her with five millilitres of cyclomorphine. This would hold back the pain and reduce the risk of vomiting.

'Where does it seem to hurt most, Miss Fawcett?'

'Well, I've scratched my face and I don't seem to be able to move my arm.'

Ruth kept her expression calm. 'No other pain or discomfort? Can you move your legs? No pain in the body?'

'Well, I did manage to walk here,' Miss Fawcett pointed out with just a touch of schoolmistressy irritation. 'I think it's only my arm and face.'

'Right. Now take my hand and squeeze it. . . Good. Now I'll lift your forearm—that hurts? Right. Now try to bend your arm. . .slowly. . .tell me when it hurts. Good. Now when I press tell me what you feel. . . I thought so.'

'Is it broken?'

'Almost certainly. In hospital they'll X-ray it, but for the moment I'll just put a sling on to immobilise it.' Quickly she opened her box and rummaged for a sling. 'This shouldn't take too long.'

Expertly Ruth fitted the sling. She thought with a half-smile that the first aid lectures she'd been shanghaied into giving to local youth groups were at last proving useful. Many doctors were poor with bandages. It was a nurse's job!

There was a tap on the door and Micah entered. He said, 'Nothing life-threatening wrong with the kids. Mostly shock with bruises, abrasions, one or two nasty cuts. None of them has any medical condition we need worry about too much. One has two fingers I think are dislocated—I'd like your opinion on them—'

'What about Mr Moody?' Miss Fawcett broke in. 'He was screaming; why haven't the police brought him here?'

'Mr Moody?' questioned Micah.

It was Angela who answered. 'He's caught under the minibus and they're trying to get him out. There's blood all over.'

'Can you cope here, Ruth? I think I ought to go and see if they need help.'

She looked at him. The once immaculate doctor had gone. His hair was awry. He was in his shirtsleeves and his shirt was stained with rain, mud and blood.

But he was her Micah, with the deep voice and the green eyes and the wonderful lips. She couldn't bear for him to go!

'I think you might be better staying here,' she faltered. She had lost one man in an accident in the mountains. She didn't want to lose another.

He knew exactly what she was thinking. 'You can manage without me, Ruth,' he said. 'There's half a dozen policemen working up there. I'm going to stand back and offer advice. I'm certainly not going to risk my life or do anything stupid.'

'I couldn't stand it if you—'

To the evident interest of both Angela and Miss Fawcett, he silenced her by bending over and kissing her briefly on the lips.

'The doctor's work is here,' he said. 'I'm going up the hill to be a spectator.'

She didn't believe a word of what he said. But he was right; there was doctor's work here and she would lose herself in it.

She was concerned about the amount of blood Miss Fawcett had lost. First she made her comfortable on the bunk, then quickly erected a Haemacell drip. When she got to hospital Miss Fawcett's blood would be cross-matched and she'd get the correct transfusion. But for the moment the Haemacell would return fluid to the blood vessels and prevent the injured teacher from going into shock. It was a temporary measure but a good one.

Then Ruth wrapped her in blankets and said she was going to look at the children.

'Are they all right?' Miss Fawcett asked, a little dreamily.

'A bit battered but yes. You did an excellent job of getting them here. Now stop worrying and I'll be right back.'

Micah had raided the food cupboard. The children were rooting through a biscuit tin, and one or two were obviously already thinking that this was a bit of an adventure. Ruth went straight to the white-faced lad who was hugging his hand to his chest.

'You're. . .Michael, is it? All right, Michael, let me see your hand.'

Reluctantly he showed her; two fingers were protruding backwards at an unmistakable angle. She held the hand gently and ran her fingers along his—just dislocations, nothing broken. Before he realised what she was doing she had seized the two fingers and pulled. The fingers clicked back into their sockets.

The lad opened his mouth to yell. She said sharply, 'Don't! That didn't hurt. Now I can see your face is grazed, but have you got any other pains?'

'I'm all right, miss,' he mumbled, and looked cautiously at his hand. 'I can move me fingers but now it hurts.'

'The worst is over,' she reassured him. 'Now let's have a look at that face.'

Angela had found a bowl and filled it with hot water. Ruth dropped a mild disinfectant into it and worked down the line, washing, cleaning with Savlodil and dressing cuts. There were no great problems. One or two children had gashes that might in time need suturing, but for the moment she dressed them with butterfly stitches.

The room was now quite warm. By the time she had finished the children were considerably more cheerful.

Instead of eight silent, miserable figures there was now a group, chatting, arguing, wondering what was going to happen next.

Angela whispered, 'I don't believe it. They're going to start causing trouble in a minute.'

'They've got a while yet. They're still suffering from shock. Can you refill that bowl and come and help me with Miss Fawcett? The hardest job is still to come.'

Miss Fawcett seemed a lot more comfortable. Ruth eased a pad under her head and then loosened the pressure bandage to look at the injured cheek. Blood flowed over her hands.

It looked as if Miss Fawcett had gashed her face on a window. There was a large V-shaped cut and the skin had pulled back to reveal the flesh underneath. The cut was dirty and Ruth could see the glint of at least one piece of glass.

That settled it. The cut would have to be X-rayed before it was finally sutured. But the bleeding was quite heavy; she would have to do something about it.

Ruth looked up to see Angela staring at the cut, white-faced. 'Policewoman Walker,' she said sharply. 'Get a drink, take a couple of deep breaths then come and hold the bowl for me. I shall need your help. D'you hear? You have to help me!'

'I'll be all right, Doctor.' A faint touch of colour came back to Angela's cheeks.

'Right, come closer.' Ruth cleaned the cut as best she could, and used forceps to ease back the skin and pull out what glass she could see. Then she used temporary sutures and finally a clamp, in the hope of slowing the bleeding.

It wasn't the job she would have done in hospital. But under the circumstances it was pretty good—and as she fixed the final suture Ruth realised she was sweating with the strain.

Angela said, 'There's somebody outside.' Ruth realised she'd subconsciously heard the sound of an engine. Perhaps it was the police. She sent Angela to check.

Another engine roared up outside and she knew it wasn't a Land Rover. Then Angela returned and Ruth blinked with surprise. Angela was followed by a soldier in battledress.

'Good afternoon, ma'am,' the soldier said. 'I'm Lieutenant McFee; we're from the camp at Calleston. Sergeant Black thought to call us. I've got two army lorries outside and a team of paramedics. How may we help?'

Hastily Ruth collected her scattered thoughts. This was the last thing she had expected. She asked, 'How did you get here?'

'We drove along the stream bed. Army lorries are expected to do that sort of thing.'

'Right, well. . .there are eight children who need to go to hospital. Nothing serious but they must be checked. I've just finished this dressing so you could take Miss Fawcett here too.'

From the bunk came an unexpectedly firm voice. 'Good afternoon, Lieutenant. I'm very pleased to see you.'

'Good afternoon, ma'am. I'll see the children are loaded at once.'

After issuing terse orders to his men the lieutenant returned. 'That's a very neat piece of work if I may say so, Doctor,' he said, gesturing to the stitched wound Ruth was covering.

'Thank you, Lieutenant, you may say so.'

He didn't seem affected by her sarcasm. He said, 'I've just returned from a tour in Northern Ireland. We see a lot of suturing there.'

She felt slightly guilty.

Two sturdy paramedics came, transferred Miss Fawcett's drip, and gently lifted her onto a stretcher. Watching their assured movements, Ruth had no hesitation in handing over her charges. These men were good.

She squeezed Miss Fawcett's hand and told her she'd soon be in hospital. The children were loaded into the lorry and firmly strapped into place. Then the great vehicle set off down the stream bed and Ruth heard a radio operator calling ahead.

'There's another problem,' she said to Lieutenant McFee.

# CHAPTER TEN

RUTH had deliberately made herself concentrate on her medical work; all thoughts of Micah had been banished. But now medical responsibility had been taken out of her hands. It was obvious that Lieutenant McFee and his men were far more expert and experienced at this kind of work than she was.

At long last the rain was moderating slightly. She pulled at the hood of her anorak and with Angela, the lieutenant and three of his heavily laden men she tramped up the hill towards the wrecked minibus. The lieutenant had suggested that she and Angela stay behind; both had told him vehemently that there was no chance of that.

She had to find Micah. She was tired, soaked, had been working in makeshift conditions treating people who could have been dangerously injured. Fortunately they weren't. But the sight of those woebegone creatures had made her realise something with blinding clarity. All life was a risk. Two hours ago none of them had dreamed they'd be involved in a crash. She realised this now and she had to find Micah to tell him. She was willing to take a risk. It could be too late, a tiny nagging thought kept telling her, but she ignored it.

They topped a ridge and ahead of them was the wrecked minibus. Quickly she surveyed the scene: two police Land Rovers backed up nearby, the long scar in the earth where the road had crumbled away, the minibus on its side, the scattered hooded police.

She heard shouts and the revving of engines and with a thrill of horror realised what was happening. The police Land Rovers were connected by ropes to the side of the minibus. They crept gently forward, the ropes tightened and the minibus started to rock. 'Micah!' she cried. He was crouched low beneath the rusty underside of the minibus. If it tipped the wrong way it would crush him.

For a moment that seemed to her an eternity, the minibus was poised. Then, with a rattle, it rolled over onto its back. Micah could be seen clearly now, kneeling over a mud-stained body. With the others she ran forward, to see his hands pressing high on the man's arm to stop the bright spurt of arterial blood from a long, contused gash.

One of the paramedics carefully moved her away. 'Let me, ma'am, this is our trade,' he said as he unslung his pack. To Micah he said, 'Just hold that pressure a moment longer, sir.'

Micah looked up in surprise, then nodded as the paramedic swiftly bound a field dressing on the damaged arm.

The other two paramedics were assembling a collapsible stretcher, attaching a portable drip. Micah looked at the lieutenant and Ruth called, 'Let them get on with it, Micah. They're experts.' She heard him talk for a moment to the lieutenant and then the stretcher with the injured man was carried into the mist as the lieutenant, Ruth, Micah and Sergeant Black gathered together.

Lieutenant McFee spoke first. 'If you're sure there's

no one else injured I'd like to get away at once. That man needs a hospital.'

Roger Black looked questioningly at Ruth. 'The others have already gone,' she said.

'No one needs a lift?' The lieutenant smiled and then said, 'I'll be in touch tonight, Sergeant.'

'Paperwork,' Roger Black said heavily. 'It's the hardest part of the job.' The lieutenant raised his hand in salute and was gone.

For a moment the three left stood in silence. For the past two hours they had worked non-stop. Now the emergency was over and they all felt a curious sense of loss.

Roger Black said formally, 'I must thank you both, Dr North and Dr Francis. We'll wrap up what we can here, go and tidy the hut and then get back home. There'll be form-filling and letters and so on and I'm afraid you'll get your share. But it'll all wait till tomorrow. Now, d'you want us to drive you home? There's room in the Land Rovers.'

Ruth said, 'We'd like to take the Range Rover back.' Then she had a thought and turned to Micah to ask anxiously, 'Are you all right? Are you fit to drive?'

'I'm wet and I'm hungry,' he said, 'but other-wise fine.'

'One of my men will walk you down to the hut,' the sergeant said, 'and thanks again.'

She felt a great urge to tell the sergeant that she felt she should thank him. Because of what he'd put her through she'd learned something. But she didn't. She didn't want to explain. They stumbled after the police-man across the slippery grass, down towards the hut.

When the path grew flatter she reached out and grasped Micah's hand.

There were a few things to collect from the hut. The policeman assured them that the hut would be put in order, and that Sergeant Black would get in touch with the club secretary. Within a few minutes Micah was helping Ruth into the passenger seat of the Range Rover, then swung himself inside and switched on the heater.

The powerful vehicle started its jerky journey down the path. She looked at her watch; it was only half past seven. Trickles of rain ran down inside her clothes and off her anorak onto the seat. 'I'm sorry to ruin your upholstery,' she said, and burst into tears.

He knew enough not to say anything. Instead he stopped the car, reached over and pulled her to him. He was cold and wet and she wouldn't have been anywhere else in the world. He smelled of mud and damp cloth but underneath was the warmth of his body and his beating heart. For a moment she was content.

But they couldn't stay here for ever. Her sobbing grew less and after a while she pushed him away gently. 'We're parked in the middle of a stream,' she pointed out.

'So we are.' The car drove forward. 'Where would you like to go?'

'Will you take me home, please?' It suddenly struck her that he was unusually silent. Perhaps he didn't feel the same way as she did. Perhaps the hug he had just given her had not been the hug of a lover, but the affectionate response of a friend. She was warmer now, but the thought chilled her.

They were passing through the little ravine that had

so upset her before. She looked at the rain-streaked rocks looming high above them. Before she had felt them to be menacing; now they were comforting, almost like old friends. Micah glanced at her sideways. 'Do they still worry you?'

She shook her head. 'No. I don't think they ever will again. This evening's changed me, Micah; I'm still getting used to some new ideas.'

'Go on,' he said as she paused. 'See if you can talk about them.'

She frowned. 'When I saw you underneath that minibus, and the police trying to turn it over, I had this sick feeling. It was all happening again. The man I . . . someone I cared for was risking his life and I was going to be left behind.'

'"Someone I cared for"?' he queried. 'What were you going to say first?'

'Never mind that,' she said firmly. 'Anyway, why did you have to stay there? It was dangerous!'

'It wasn't too dangerous. Sergeant Black and I checked the Land Rovers carefully. There was only a minimal risk.'

'Why couldn't you just stand back while they pulled the minibus off him?'

'There was a torn piece of metal stuck in the man's arm; it had cut the artery. Fortunately his clothing made a compress, which slowed the blood loss. But I knew that I had to stop the arterial bleeding as soon as the metal was pulled out. He'd still lost a lot of blood.'

'I see,' she said. She did understand. He had taken a risk—but it had been a carefully worked out one.

'Now it's your turn to explain,' he said cheerfully.

'Just before, were you going to say "the man I loved was risking his life"?'

There was a moment's silence, and she realised that this question was a tiny test. She had made some kind of decision to change her life, to be more open with herself, less guarded with other people. Could she carry it through?

'Yes,' she said. 'I was going to say the man I loved.'

'And by that you meant me?'

She was trying to change, but he mustn't expect too much too quickly. 'Don't push me too hard,' she said. 'I've spent years being cautious in what I've said and what I've done. You'll have to wait.'

He reached over and ran his fingers down her damp cheek and her skin burned under the delicate caress. 'I think you're wonderful,' he said. 'I'll try to wait— but I don't know if I can.'

Without giving her time to speak he went on, 'It's time for some music. And I know just the piece I want to hear.'

'What is it?' she asked, reaching to the rack of tapes. 'I'll put it on.'

'The last movement of Beethoven's Ninth Symphony.'

'The "Hymn to Joy"?'

'It's the way I feel.'

She didn't speak for a while after that. She was content to sit and listen as the great music swelled inside the car and the rattle of rain outside provided a counterpoint. She felt that everything would be well. For different reasons this had been one of the most exhausting days of her life. She glanced at her watch. And it was still only seven forty-five.

The car stopped outside her door and she said to him, 'I want you to come in. You're not going back to the Bell like that.'

At first he didn't move and she felt a faint sense of misgiving. 'You do want to come in, don't you?' she ventured.

'You can't guess just how much I do. But Ruth, you've had a hard day. Perhaps you ought to rest. You might do—or say—things that you might regret afterwards—'

'Shut up and get in that house,' she interrupted. 'I know exactly what I'm doing and I want no argument.'

'Lord save me from bossy doctors,' she heard him mutter.

She was used to coming in wet through. In the porch of her cottage there were pegs for drenched coats and a tray for footwear. But they were both still soaked as they squelched into her living room.

'This is my home and you're my guest,' she said. 'Now get upstairs and have a bath. There are towels in the cupboard. Dump your wet clothes in the plastic basket and we'll see about cleaning them later. I'll find you something to wear.'

He didn't move at once. Instead he reached out, took an escaped strand of her hair and ran his fingers along it. 'Look at you,' he said. 'Your hair isn't neat and precise and exact any more. Your tracksuit's wet through and sticking to you and I can see far more of your body than you think you're showing. You look a mess and you look gorgeous.' He leaned forward and kissed her briefly on the lips.

'Bath,' she shouted. 'And before you get in it take

a look at yourself. You're no picture of elegance. I'll phone Harry and report in. He'll be worrying about us.'

'OK, I'm going.' He lifted his hands in surrender.

It seemed odd to think that Harry and Martin might still be at the surgery. She got through to Harry, who was pleased to hear from her and told her that Sergeant Black had phoned. He'd said that the police couldn't have managed without the two of them and everything was now under control. Harry said that she and Micah didn't need to come into the surgery the next day.

'Rubbish,' Ruth said tartly. 'We're only wet, not injured. We'll both be there as usual.'

'I knew suggesting it was a waste of time.' Harry rang off.

She went to her bedroom, dropped her sodden clothes in a basket and pulled on an old dressing gown. It suddenly struck her that she was famished, and Micah must feel the same. They both needed food as fuel—and quickly.

Hastily she tipped two tins of thick soup into a sauce-pan and set it ready to warm. Then she cut and buttered bread and brought out Stilton, Cheddar and Brie. Lastly she made two mugs of tea. From a cupboard she took a rarely used bottle of whisky and poured a generous slug in the mug intended for Micah. She carried the mug upstairs and tapped on the bathroom door.

'I'm leaving a mug of tea for you outside the door.'

To her surprise the door opened. Micah was framed there, a towel wrapped loosely round his waist, but the rest of him undeniably naked. About him was the faint smell of her best ivory soap. Uncertainly her gaze travelled over his broad shoulders, the flat stomach, the two great wings of hair that fanned over his chest. There seemed such a lot of him and he was so obviously male.

'I had a shower,' he said, 'but I filled the bath for you. I didn't like to think of you wet and uncomfortable.'

She felt tongue-tied. 'Well, thanks,' she mumbled. 'I was going to. . .'

He took the tea from her, moved out and pressed her gently into the bathroom. 'Thanks for the drink; it's exactly what I want.' He lifted the mug and sniffed. 'Whisky-flavoured tea? What will they think of next?' The door clicked shut behind him.

It was her bathroom; she'd designed it and she loved it. Her plants grew on the window-sill, and she'd picked the orange curtains and the matching carpet. Although she was now warmer, she realised she was tired and grubby. The bath looked so inviting. She threw in a capsule of expensive bath oil, unpinned her hair, dropped her dressing gown on the floor then stepped in. It was bliss!

She lay there, content to let the heat soak away the stress and pains. She'd read somewhere that the finest discovery of civilisation was a hot bath; she thought she agreed.

There was a click and a voice said, 'I've brought your tea.'

She squeaked and sat up—then folded her arms over her breasts and sank below water level again. She watched as, still clad only in the towel, Micah sat on her bathroom stool.

'You'd forgotten to put the whisky in your tea,' he

said conversationally, 'so I did it for you. Here, have a drink.'

'You're in my bathroom,' she pointed out.

'So I am. I've got you trapped. Just for once you're not working, thinking or having to go somewhere. We can talk.'

'Talk! I was looking forward to twenty minutes' peace!'

'That's a lovely idea. We'll sit here and enjoy it together.'

'But I'm. . .well, I'm in the bath; I've got no clothes on.'

'All I'm wearing is this rather skimpy towel. You're quite adequately covered by all that foam.'

She wasn't going to win this argument. 'Well, pass me my tea, then,' she grumbled and stretched out a hand. She didn't want him coming too close.

For a while she lay there, eyes closed, sipping her tea, the hot, scented water rippling over her shoulders. A languorous warmth spread through her body. The knotted tensions of the day slowly dissolved and she felt happy and relaxed. She even liked having a practically naked man in her bathroom.

That fact must have communicated itself to him somehow. Rising from the stool, he knelt by the side of the bath and leaned his forearm on the edge. She felt disturbed; he seemed very close.

'If you sit up,' he said, 'I'll wash your back.'

The very idea! Her first reaction was to sink even deeper below the surface. But then she realised that it was too late for modesty. Besides, this was the new, risk-taking Ruth and if they were to have a relationship she'd have to put something into it. 'All right,' she said.

No one had washed her back since she was a little girl. It was comforting to sit there, feeling strong hands rub and stroke and rinse.

'I've never seen you with your hair down,' he said. 'It's so long.'

'My one concession to femininity. It would make more sense to have it cut, but I've always had it like this.'

'You mustn't cut it.' He lifted her hair over her shoulder and smoothed it downwards.

'That's not my back,' she said tartly.

He was unabashed. 'I know. But it's still very nice.' Then he leaned over to kiss the damp nape of her neck and like a cat she arched her back in pleasure.

'For a nice conventional doctor you make love in some strange places,' he said. 'A garden or a moor or a bathroom.'

'We are not making love. I'm having a bath and you're. . .you're. . .'

'Now what am I doing? I wonder.' Abruptly he stood, putting soap and flannel on the side of the bath. 'This towel's a bit brief, Ruth. Have you anything else I could wear?'

She was disappointed. His voice was still pleasant but his mood had somehow changed. 'If you look on the left-hand side of my wardrobe you'll see a red tracksuit hanging up. I bought it but it's far too big for me.'

'Thanks. See you downstairs, then?' And he was gone.

I mustn't rush things, she thought, and reached for the shower attachment to rinse her hair.

Ten minutes later she hesitantly walked into her

living room. She wore a silk dressing gown in a rich dark green colour and a towel was knotted in a turban round her hair.

When she saw Micah she had to laugh. The tracksuit was far too big for her, but far too small for him. The trousers only came down to the middle of his calf and the jacket was stretched across his shoulders and wouldn't meet across his chest. 'You look like Sinbad,' she cried.

'I know. I think I've let a genie out of a bottle and it's going to give me whatever I want.'

'So what are you going to ask for?'

He took her hand and led her to the table. 'We're both doctors. We know our blood-sugar level is down. The first thing we do is be sensible and eat.'

'What's the second thing we do?'

'We'll see what the genie brings us.'

She hadn't realised how hungry she was. The meal she'd quickly prepared was perfect and afterwards they sat on her settee, each holding a glass of wine and staring into the fire.

'Doctors are trained not to be emotional,' he said.

She corrected him. 'Not to be *too* emotional—or emotional about the wrong things. I think too many doctors have rackety private lives because they don't feel enough. Too many of them drink, for a start.'

'True. And we two aren't much better. You lost your husband and it made you less ready to take emotional risks. You cut yourself off from an entire set of feelings. . .'

'No, I didn't!' she burst out. 'I loved him and I was hurt and I thought I never wanted to suffer that again.'

'Things pass in time,' he said gently. 'Even pain.'

He didn't come closer to her but reached out for her hand. It was comforting having her hand held.

After a while she admitted to herself that he was right. The pain of Matt's death had passed; she just hadn't realised it. With the knowledge came a sense of relief. 'I suppose you're right.'

'I've not been much better. When I was a financier I had to maintain a stony face. The mask was always necessary. If you lost, no one had to guess. And I suppose old habits die hard.'

After a moment's silence he went on, 'Now I'm changing. I love you. I think I've loved you since I first saw you that day in the surgery. I couldn't believe it; you were like a vision and you were annoyed with me. I would have done anything to make you smile.'

She felt bewildered, but tried to remember. 'I thought your voice was very attractive,' she offered, 'and I was so pleased when. . .when you looked as wonderful as you sounded. Did you say you loved me?'

'I did and I do. Remember Goose Hall?'

'I could fall for that house,' she said.

'Well, I told you there that I wanted us to wait and see what happened between us. That was stupid. What's happened between us is the best thing in my life, and I know it. I love you, Ruth, and I want you now.'

She felt her heart pounding. In front of her a new life was unfolding, new hopes, new prospects. She realised she'd been living in a cold, self-enclosing shell—and this man would show her the way out. 'I'm still a bit frightened,' she said timidly, 'but I want to try.'

'I'm frightened myself, my darling,' he said. 'I've never felt like this before.'

As he'd spoken, he'd been moving closer to her. Now his arms reached round her and pulled her to him. She received his kisses willingly.

For a while she was content just to sit there, her arms clutched round him as he kissed her throat, her cheek, her forehead and then, lovingly, her lips. His hand caressed her cheek, stroked her neck and then eased aside the folds of her gown so that he could cup her breast. His head bent so that his tongue could touch the aroused, hard pink tip and she gasped with pleasure.

Now she could—she would risk all. She panted, 'You said we've made love in a garden, on a moor and in a bathroom. Now I want you to make love to me on my bed.'

He lifted his head and she trembled at the sight of the desire smouldering in his eyes. 'Are you sure you. . .?' he muttered huskily, and she held her hand to his mouth.

'I'm sure. Now take me to my bed.'

Hand in hand they went upstairs. It was dusk now and she switched on the dim bedside light. Then she threw off her gown and dragged the towel from round her hair. Naked, she gazed at him.

With a few swift movements he tore off the tracksuit so that he too was naked. Then he crushed her to him. She could feel his masculinity, sense the strength and passion in him, and knew there would be no reserve. She revelled in him, in the force she had unleashed.

He was strong; he lifted her and laid her on the bed. 'Ruth,' he groaned, but again she pressed her hand to his lips.

'Don't talk now,' she whispered. 'I want you.'

For a while longer he kissed her naked body and she groaned and writhed under the sweet torture. But then she felt his growing need and she pulled him to her, and then, with a soft moan, into her.

Joined by their love, they clung to each other, moving in an ecstasy of pleasure. Then she felt his passion soaring to a peak and joined him with a wild cry as his love flooded through her.

Then it was over. But as they lay there, side by side, face to face, his leg across her body, there was a contentment as deep as their passion had been high.

'We took a risk,' he said.

'We'll take another one soon,' she replied.

# MILLS & BOON

## Back by Popular Demand

# BETTY NEELS

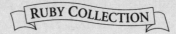

RUBY COLLECTION

**A collector's edition of forty favourite titles from one of the world's best-loved romance authors.**

Mills & Boon are proud to bring back these sought after titles, now reissued in beautifully matching volumes and presented together in one cherished collection.

Don't miss these unforgettable titles, coming next month:

Title #1    THE DOUBTFUL MARRIAGE
Title #2    A GEM OF A GIRL

Available wherever
Mills & Boon books are sold

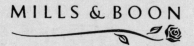

# MILLS & BOON

## MEDICAL ROMANCE

### LOVE ON CALL

**The books for enjoyment this month are:**

| | |
|---|---|
| **BUSH DOCTOR'S BRIDE** | Marion Lennox |
| **FORGOTTEN PAIN** | Josie Metcalfe |
| **COUNTRY DOCTORS** | Gill Sanderson |
| **COURTING DR GROVES** | Meredith Webber |

### Treats in store!

Watch next month for the following absorbing stories:

| | |
|---|---|
| **TENDER TOUCH** | Caroline Anderson |
| **LOVED AND LOST** | Margaret Barker |
| **THE SURGEON'S DECISION** | Rebecca Lang |
| **AN OLD-FASHIONED PRACTICE** | Carol Wood |

Available from W.H. Smith, John Menzies, Volume One,
Forbuoys, Martins, Woolworths, Tesco, Asda, Safeway and
other paperback stockists.

Readers in South Africa - write to:
IBS, Private Bag X3010, Randburg 2125.

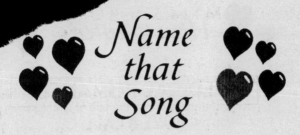

# Name that Song

How would you like to win a year's supply of simply irresistible romances? Well, you can and they're free! Simply solve the puzzle below and send your completed entry to us by 31st October 1996. The first five correct entries picked after the closing date will each win a years supply of Temptation novels (four books every month—worth over £100).

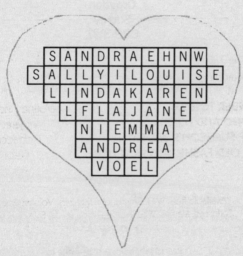

| S | A | N | D | R | A | E | H | N | W |
|---|---|---|---|---|---|---|---|---|---|
| S | A | L | L | Y | I | L | O | U | I | S | E |
| L | I | N | D | A | K | A | R | E | N |
| | L | F | L | A | J | A | N | E |
| | N | I | E | M | M | A |
| | A | N | D | R | E | A |
| | V | O | E | L |

*Please turn over for details of how to enter* ☞

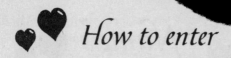

# How to enter

To solve our puzzle...first circle eight well known girls names hidden in the grid. Then unscramble the remaining letters to reveal the title of a well-known song (five words).

When you have written the song title in the space provided below, don't forget to fill in your name and address, pop this page into an envelope (you don't need a stamp) and post it today! Hurry—competition ends 31st October 1996.

**Mills & Boon Song Puzzle**
**FREEPOST**
**Croydon**
**Surrey**
**CR9 3WZ**

Song Title: _____

Are you a Reader Service Subscriber?   Yes ❏     No ❏

Ms/Mrs/Miss/Mr _____

Address _____

_____

_____ Postcode _____

One application per household.

You may be mailed with other offers from other reputable companies as a result of this application. If you would prefer not to receive such offers, please tick box.   ❏

C396
D